D0290329

Sip

Sip

Brian Allen Carr

SOHO

Published by
Soho Press, Inc.
853 Broadway
New York, NY 10003

Library of Congress Cataloging-in-Publication Data

Carr, Brian Allen, 1979–
Sip / Brian Allen Carr.

ISBN 978-1-61695-827-5
eISBN 978-1-61695-828-2

I. Title

PS3603.A772 S57 2017 813'.6—dc23 LC 2016056387

Interior design by Janine Agro, Soho Press, Inc.

Printed in the United States of America

10 9 8 7 6 5 4 3 2 1

Sip

one

They'd sip their shadows and the darkness stained them. Anyone who said they saw it coming told bad lies. There existed no concrete prophecy foretelling the malady, no rational explanation science could come to. How could it be, this new behavior? Drinking light's absence? Falling crude victim?

The religious offered up bits of texts.

From Acts and Joel and Revelations came the closest warning: "The sun will be turned to darkness and the moon to blood."

"But the moon ain't blood," skeptics argued.

"Not yet," believers said, looking up at the night sky gravely.

And then from the Al-Furqan:"But they are going to know, when they see the punishment who is farthest astray . . . Have you seen the one who takes as his god his own desire . . . Have you not considered your Lord—how He extends the shadow, and if He willed, He could have made it stationary? Then We made the sun for it an indication. Then We hold it in hand for a brief grasp."

"So it's a punishment from God?"

"Only He knows why He does His doings."

When doctors were asked to explain it, they'd invoke other anomalies *from medical history—mysteries, freak occurrences that could never be explained:*

"Strasbourg, Alsace in 1518. A woman named Frau Troffea begins dancing, can't stop. Dozens join in with her, within a month, hundreds. All of them dancing ferociously, endlessly. No one knows why, though some have blamed a kind of mass psychosis induced by stress, others suggesting ergot poisoning might have fueled the catastrophe. See, many of the dancers danced themselves to death, and it's even been said that the dancers danced beyond that. Moved on with some inaudible, internal music even postmortem. And no one is entirely certain why."

"This ain't 1518, though."

"And ain't nobody fucking dancing."

Murk

The sun was up, so the dark could start. All about the ground, all in the same direction, shadows sprawled. And this is what he was after.

Murk crept from the mesquite trees into the full light of day. Hobbling, his clothes dirty and tattered—his left leg a wooden peg. He shooed gnats from his face as he advanced, humming a bit of tune.

"A world with two suns," he sang softly, "and both are for me." It was as if his mother's breast milk had been ashes. He had thirsty-looking skin and hair thickly greased with sleep. He'd been growing it out, his hair, and wasn't used to the length of it. He constantly tucked the brown thatch behind his ears. Most his life, he'd kept it short, but he'd found an old Doors album while rummaging a capsized van, and he wanted to look like the guy on the cover. Around that time, he'd started making up songs.

He found the sun and put his back to it. He knew he should wait a few hours, let the light get brighter, his shadow darker, more potent, but the call in him could not be placated—he lacked self-control.

"I missed you," he said to his shadow on the ground. He waved. It waved back. He danced. It did too. "Lose weight?" he asked it. "Something different with your hair?" But, of course, there was no answer. "Either way," he said, "looking good."

He dropped to his knees, lowered his face to his shade-made print, now a hunched clot of dark on the grass.

"A world with two suns," he continued singing, "that is the dream."

He was silent. Lust slithered across his face. He tucked his mane behind his ears, palmed his cheeks, and motes of dry skin swirled away.

Then . . .

Down he went like a starving man. His mouth bored open, he crashed against dirt, and he gulped at the dark, each swallow dimming the shade. Murk grunted and gnashed, pulling the shadow off the ground and into his mouth, down in his belly.

When he'd gotten it all, or as much as he could gather, he rolled to his back laughing and let the magic work its charm. "A world with two suns," he bellowed, "that is the dream," his mouth as wide open as an opera singer's and his lips and teeth grayed with stain. His eyes drew black. His skin went pale. His veins showed through like sooty scribbles on pale parchment.

In the distance he could hear the train. To Murk, it was the sound of heaven.

The Train

Mira crouched, watching for the train to race around again on its mile-long, circular track. She looked for the break between the caboose and the engine to catch glimpse of the buildings beyond. A step in front of her, the grass had been scorched away, covered with white rocks, but the smell of the scorching lingered, and Mira sniffed the perfume of it, her brown eyes sleepy in the smell. She messed her hair. She'd never thought much of it, but then Murk started growing his and one day she looked at him and couldn't help but ask, "Are you trying to look like me?"

He got defensive, something about some singer.

"You're trying to steal my fucking haircut," she told him.

And Murk called Mira all kinds of dirty names and stomped off on his peg leg to wherever Murk went when Mira sent him stomping.

But now, she thought, "Shit, he can have it."

Just beyond the train, observation towers stood, and in them guards trained guns on the perimeter of rocks. Mira heard the man's voice through his bullhorn.

"Closer and I'll fire."

It was half past noon, and Mira was ambivalent. She'd been coming to the train for days now with the halfhearted idea of dying, but each time she'd come, nothing happened. This threat was the first she'd heard, and it made the consequence of her dying more real to her.

That's the thing about suicidal thinking: it's kind of harmless until it isn't.

A few days back, she'd stood motionless with a bouquet of citrus blossoms clutched to her chest, a kind of funeral service in her heart, but she'd only lingered for hours thinking she'd gone unnoticed. She'd even shown her shadow then, turning it off and on, hoping the strobe of it might gain some attention, but it didn't.

The next time, she'd gone to a different edge of the town, thinking maybe her luck would change if she tried another observation tower. Each time the train sped up, but no shots were fired. She thought mildly of running for the train, throwing herself beneath its heavy steel wheels and letting the train cars chew her up to yuck, but she couldn't seem to get her legs to go through with it.

It was puzzling. She'd been shot at before. When Murk had sent her to the train the first time. It's why she'd even come to think of this as a way out of the world. So what was different? Why weren't they firing now?

She knelt toward the rocks, lifted one of the white pebbles casually. Her tanned knees flecked with scars, her palms rough from hard work and living. She dropped the rock, contemplated the white dust it left behind on her. She blew at it and most of the stuff disappeared, and what was left she licked away, spat out at the grass, and the chalky flavor of the task left a scowl on her face.

"What now, Mira?" she asked herself, her words aimed at the train. "What happens next?"

Guards

In the observation tower, the guard shouldered his gun. He brought the sight of the weapon to his eye, set the crosshair on her forehead. The girl mouthed something but he couldn't tell what. He liked the look of her brick-colored lips, how they spoke the inaudible words. He pretended a voice for her, to match the look she had: a bauble that's shatterproof, a wild kind of preciousness.

"Same girl as yesterday?" asked Drummond.

"And the day before," said Bale. "And the day before that." He chewed at nothing, his perfect teeth click-clicking a toneless music.

"How she know what tower you'll be at? I mean, we draw y'all's names from a hat even. Ain't no order to it at all."

"Don't know," said Bale. "First time she came, she had flowers."

"Flowers?" Drummond and Bale were brothers and both had the same pretty teeth. They had a large, domestic build, as though they'd been bred rather than born.

"Bunch of white ones, but that ain't even the strangest part."

"Shoot her. It's too screwy."

"Wait," said Bale. "Wait and watch." He stretched his neck. Rolled his thick shoulders. Smiled a childish grin.

They both wore white fatigues. They had both entered duty at the age of sixteen, as had most of the lower-ranked members of their outpost. Drummond, entered a year before Bale, was Bale's superior, but they'd both spent the last thirteen months working the train slowly across the countryside to this spot—the train operating across a length of track only slightly longer than itself, inching forward and then resting as the section of traversed track was disassembled and then reassembled in front of the engine to begin again the laggard cycle.

When the captain decided, those straight rails were recycled, used in the building of the observation towers—one of which Drummond and Bale now stood in—new curved rails were produced from cargo cars and laid ahead of the train as it progressed into its permanent circular orbit. And there they were: perhaps a hundred miles from the safety of the dome, forging some in between life.

"You should shoot," Drummond said. He picked up a radio and ordered the train to increase its speed for protection. The train always rode its circular track, a kind of moving wall around them, a millipede in pursuit of itself. "She might not be alone."

"There," said Bale, who'd stayed watching the girl.

Drummond turned the binoculars to her. "Alright?" said Drummond. "She's kinda pretty, right? Like a dark little fairy. Or like that story about that soup Indian. Remember that one? That guy lost in the wilderness. Pocahontas or some shit?"

"I don't mean that," said Bale. "Look at the ground."

"What the hell is that?"

"Keep watching."

They both stood still. The train's wheels screeched and chirped across the track. Bale peeked through the scope of his rifle, Drummond through his binoculars. "It's like pulsing," said Drummond. "Gotta be an illusion, right?"

"Maybe," said Bale, "but you ever seen an illusion like it?"

"Should've just shot the first time you saw her."

"She was holding flowers, man. It's hard to kill a pretty thing holding flowers."

"Well don't shoot now." He handed the binoculars to Bale. "We should at least see what the captain has to say on it."

They had seen shadows on the white rocks before, cast from the folks they'd shot, people who had come toward the train with their arms held high. But they had never seen a shadow that could come and go as it pleased.

Mira Meets Bale

Mira lifted another white rock from the mess of them. She rolled it in her hand, contemplated its weight. It was a jagged little thing, and she clenched it in her fist.

Back home, Mira's mother sat in her sickness. By now, she'd be curious why Mira hadn't returned. She'd be calling out raggedly for her, wallowing in the darkness, her sleepless mind addled and angry.

Mira opened her hand. The rock cast a meager shadow against her palm. She shook her head, dropped it and it clicked against the other stones a few times before coming to rest.

"No one could blame you," she said to herself. "Get up. Go forward. Get shot. Mom does whatever Mom does. Murk probably makes up a stupid song about you." She stood and moved toward the train, across the white rocks, crunching as she stepped.

The glinting steel wheels turned endlessly, were polished by friction. The noise of the moving locomotive pulsed a rhythm, and beneath that pulse, a mild squeal of steel against steel.

The closer Mira got, the more she could make out the man in

the tower. He was cleaner than anyone she'd ever seen, his clothes newer.

He had his rifle on her, and she closed her eyes, walked on toward the sound.

Her heart raced. She figured each step to be her last. Any second a bullet would catch her. But, when the noise of the train was nearly on her, when she could taste the acrid rust off the cars, smell the tangy sun-warmed metal, she opened her eyes, gazed up at the watchtower.

"You waiting for something?" Mira asked.

"Waiting?" came the answer. Both nearly shouting over the noise of the train.

"Earlier," Mira said. "You told me closer and I'll fire. I'm closer."

"My orders changed."

"Your orders changed? That was like two minutes ago."

Bale checked his watch. "Closer to five."

"Either way." She held out her arms. Scowled up at Bale. She wore denim shorts, a brown, sleeveless T-shirt, shoes that appeared homemade. "You'd be doing me a favor."

Bale adjusted his rifle grip. "Wait, you wanna get shot?"

"None a your damn business." Her eyes closed.

"Here's the deal. Right now, I'm not shooting because I was told not to. Where's your flowers?"

"Flowers?" Her eyes opened.

"The other day," said Bale. "White ones."

"I didn't . . ."

"And that blinking shadow you had?"

Mira's mouth agape.

"Getting shot probably hurts like a motherfucker. You know that right?"

Mira's confusion written in her expression.

"Like the bullet going through you and all. I got stabbed with a pencil once. In my back. That was the worst. Thing stuck in there. I walked around for twenty minutes that way until I found someone to pull it out. Still got the scar, if you wanna see. Probably can't really make it out from down there though." There was probably thirty feet between them.

"I want you to shoot."

"Nope," said Bale. "Orders. What's your name?"

She seemed to spit breath. "I ain't telling you, domer."

"C'mon," he said. "Make you a deal. Tell me your name, and I'll think about shooting you."

She snarled up at him. "Mira," she said.

Bale blinked slow. "Thought about it. Mine's Bale. How'd you know where I'd be?"

"Where you'd be?"

"Yup. Past three days you've come to my tower. You got magic?"

"Magic?"

"Shit, I don't even know where I'm going till I get there."

Mira put her hands to her face. "Figures," she said. She turned. She began to walk away.

"Wait," hollered Bale. "Where you going?"

But Mira didn't answer.

She worked her way back across the white rocks and into the brush, went dejectedly from one clutch of trees to the next. The light of day was graying and now she had to fetch dark for her mom. She stomped off toward home.

In a field of yellowed grass she saw two boys so she hid up in some briars. Her arms caught on the thorns of them, but she wanted to be careful. The boys were laughing at whatever, and she figured they had black eyes. The wind was steady. They spoke, but Mira couldn't make out their words. One of them cackled and the other belched up some response. He bloomed his form. Stretched out like putty. Shadow sippers could do it. They could stretch out like balloons, become light like paper, float like leaves. And that's what they both did, bounced along like astronauts on the moon.

Once she was sure they couldn't see her, Mira ran into the field. She stopped. Eyed the sky. Between her and the sun, a black vulture passed, its wings extended and still. It happened fast. A fortune for certain. The shadow of the bird swung across her face, and she grabbed a mouthful of it, her cheeks bulged with the thickness of its shade.

She had stolen the shadow from enough animals to understand the bird felt it. She'd never stolen from carrion crows. They usually flew too high, weren't between her and the sun, but she knew doves well. Rabbits. Squirrels. She didn't like to take from mice, because sometimes you'd take the whole thing, and she understood the horror that brought them. How they'd never sleep on their own again.

The animals she knew well could tell her, in their way, in their language of mixed sounds and stares, that it felt like a whisper coming off their hearts. She felt guilty about it but had no choice.

Mira ran full cheeked into her thicket, through the low-limbed trees and to the little house where her mother sat on the porch, her feet propped on an ancient, unplugged television set.

"What took so long?" her mother asked, her face pale and eyes strained, her posture the shape of illness.

Mira didn't answer. She lowered her face to her mother's. The two touched lips. Mira exhaled the pilfered shadow into her, and, almost instantly, her mother fell asleep.

Drummond

Captain Flamsteed wore wire-rimmed glasses, had a face like a bird and the crown of his head was shiny bald.

"Off and on?" he said again. "You're sure? This is highly preposterous even for out here. It doesn't jive with the literature we've accumulated. I'm reluctant to assume you're correct." He stood behind a desk. Jostled papers. It seemed his mind was elsewhere.

Drummond shifted. "I'm sure that's what my eyes saw, but I'm not sure I trust 'em."

"I'll appreciate if you follow me now." Flamsteed led Drummond into the sun. He contemplated the ground. "Spread your legs," he said, and Drummond did. "Arms out at your side." Again, Drummond followed orders. Flamsteed investigated Drummond's shadow.

"I'm not on it," said Drummond.

"Under circumstances such as these, I'd suggest speaking when spoken to."

"Yes, sir. It's just . . ."

"The notion that you were reluctant to shoot the creature is positively absurd."

"I suggested it to my guard."

"Suggested? Doesn't that seem mild? You are his superior."

"I told him it was protocol."

"It is most certainly that."

"There was debate about it."

"Ridiculous. Why would the matter be given any consideration beyond ensuring true aim?"

"We thought you should be informed. On account of the blinking."

Flamsteed stomped. "Ridiculous," he said again.

The only sound was the train's eternal circling—a pulse made by machinery, a bizarre preaching of friction. Chugga-chugga whee. It went. Chuck-chugga whee-chugga.

Mira and Her Mother

Mira's mother woke later, mouthy and alert, sort of annoyed. "What was that you gave me? The dreams spun circles."

"Buzzard." She was sitting in a chair near her mother, peeling carrots with a knife, dragging the blade across the dirtied skin of them. "You like birds."

"But buzzard?" said her mother. "Shit. Them things are rats with wings. Lucky I didn't dream of rotten dog ass."

"So lucky," Mira said. She finished up, dried her knife with a rag.

"I can't believe it."

"The sun was going down. Was all I could find."

"I'm just a chore to you, aren't I?"

"Stop."

Mira made to stand and go inside to the kitchen

"I wish I wasn't, but I'm a brutal chore."

"You're my mother."

"Exactly. And it should be me taking care of you. But it ain't worked out like that."

"You do, kind of."

"How?"

Mira thought better of answering. She set her knife and her bowl of carrots on top of the broke-down TV. "Tell me what brings the best dreams?" She sat back down.

Her mother understood. "You see," she said, "you can't even answer me."

"What brings the best dreams and tomorrow I'll find it. Then maybe you'll feel better, and drop all this."

Mira's mother's eyes flashed lethal. "Seagulls bring dreams of water. Squirrels, the limbs of trees. Eternities of them. Thickets and thickets. Rabbit shadows make me dream about holes and nooks and tunnels, but not in a bad way. It's warm. Before, when I could sleep my own sleep, I'd dream of home, which sounds like it would be good, but it wasn't. I'd dream your father's face, and it only broke my heart. You have his face but my manner, so it gladdens me, and if I could dream your face, it'd comfort me, but I can't, and you can't understand."

Mira just waited for the real answer to come.

"Water," her mother finally said. "Water's a good thing to dream over. Multitudes of it. Vast expanses. Every direction. Endless. What about a gull? Is that asking too much?"

"A gull?" said Mira. "I can try."

"You sure?"

"I suppose."

"I don't want to be a burden." She touched Mira's smooth chin with her fingers, her skin the color of pecan wood.

"I know." Mira said a little prayer in her mind that a gull would come her way from the coast, the prayer sort of dancing in her eyes.

"What about tonight?" said her mother.

"What about it?"

Mira's mother took a book from beside her. An almanac. She set it in her lap and it fell open to a marked page. She read. "Moon's out, just waning."

Mira laughed. "You want me to find a gull tonight?"

Her mother tried laughing too. "No. No."

"Good."

"Not a gull." Her mother could sense Mira's sorrow at the request. She flashed her teeth as though pained, the ruinous color of them off-putting. "It can be just anything," she said. "Just try an hour. If you can't find anything, come home."

"Really?"

"I'm a burden, I know. The whole world's a mess. You would've loved to know me before. When you were inside me. Or even just before all this."

"I did know you before."

"You weren't but a child. And look at you now. Basically a lady. You never saw me with adult eyes. You saw me as a child sees its mother. With eyes that hadn't learned to judge."

"I don't judge you."

"Not meaning to," said her mother. "It can't be helped. I bet the errands I send you on make you mad enough to cuss."

"I never cuss," said Mira.

"Sure."

"Never about that."

"Fine."

Mira wasn't ready to go back out so she made to change the subject. "I went to the train today."

Her mom had fidgety fingers. "You crazy? Wanting to get killed? Way Murk tells it, they shoot our kind."

"Not today," said Mira. "Even spoke to one of them domers."

"Spoke to one?"

"Named Bale."

"Well?"

"Well what?"

"Don't act dumb. What'd he say? Why they out here even?"

"It didn't get to all that."

"What'd it get to?"

Mira took the book from her mother's lap, set it off to the side, hoped it wouldn't be picked up again. "He had orders not to shoot me, and he wanted to know my name. That was about it."

"You didn't ask him about fixing it?"

"Fixing it?"

"When they went in there, in them domes. That was supposed to be part of it. Figuring out how to get stolen shadows back. And not with toad licking and burying pubic hair at midnight and everything else I tried. Eating hand sanitizer. Moonshine eye drops. They were supposed to fix it with medicine."

"It didn't come up."

"How could it not've?"

"I'd other things on my mind."

"You gotta go back."

"Now?"

Her mom shook her head. "Course not."

"Good."

"But tomorrow."

Mira was silent.

"Promise." She grabbed up one of Mira's hands, held it between her palms as though praying with it. "And this time, ask."

Mira pulled away. "I'm busy tomorrow."

"Doing what?"

"Looking for a gull."

"Oh, forget that gull a bit. This is important. They know how to fix this, you won't have to be looking for any shadows for me no more no how."

Mira considered it. What if it could be fixed? What if her mother could get her shadow back and sleep again on her own, dream her own dreams? Wouldn't that solve most everything? Would she even want to get shot at the train then? "Okay," she said. "I'll try."

"Good," said her mom. "Be back in an hour?"

"An hour?"

"Yeah, don't stay gone more. And it can be anything," she said. "Anything but a cat. They have absurd dreams, leaves me puzzled. A bunch of touching the same thing over and over just to know that it's there. Looking around and wondering what to pee on."

"Oh," said Mira. "For tonight."

"Yes, for tonight," she said. "You'd understand if it was you. It's not fair for either of us, but it's less fair for me."

"Okay," said Mira, and she walked barefoot away from their house and back out into the thicket of mesquite and into the moonlight, and, as soon as she was far enough away that her mother couldn't hear her, she made fists, and, "This is bullshit," she said.

Bale

Captain Flamsteed asked again, "Please walk me through the logic of your decision."

Bale thought about it. Replayed it in his mind. "I thought Drummond told you. The shadow. Thought someone should know."

"Someone did know," said Flamsteed. "You were well aware of every portion of the puzzle at hand. She came to the warning track. She was not one of ours. It's really pretty plain. In every training procedure you've undergone, the rules of your post have been broadcast to you loud and clear. Shoot to kill. Those are the orders."

"In Bale's defense," Drummond said, "it was peculiar."

"These shadow-sucking vagrants with their blackened eyes and hearts. These people with their horrific, damnable minds. Has some part of you become sorry for them?"

"Not at all," said Bale. "It was just out of the ordinary." He rubbed a hand across his short brown hair.

"Have you forgotten what they're capable of?"

Bale had never seen it, but he'd heard it told. "No, sir," he said. "I could never forget."

Night Hunting

Mira couldn't figure why her mother cared where the sleep came from. They kept chickens, rabbits, and goats, but Mira's mother forbade that. "We take enough from them already," she'd said. They ate them and milked them and stole their eggs. But, when it came to shadows, Mira's mother drew the line.

It hadn't always been that way.

Mira was young when her mother had her shadow swallowed off her, and, back then, Mira couldn't hunt out on her own. Her mother would send her into the yard to get mouthfuls of chicken shade so she could rest on the porch, swallow that dream of feathers and noise.

Mira brought her home the shadow of a wild bird once, she couldn't even remember what kind, and after that things began to change. Her mother would request certain shadows, and sometimes Mira could find them. Either way, her days and nights were spent on these ridiculous errands—the moon-made shadows less potent, but still.

Only creatures with consciousness worked in this regard,

though Mira's mother regretted it. "Can you imagine the sleep bluebonnets would lead you to? Dreams of meadows and sun, soft breezes. Or sunflowers? Head high in a warm prairie? The smell of grass and all that sky?"

"Or cactus?" said Mira.

"Cactus? No no. That could only bring thorny dreams."

"Yup," said Mira. "Safe thorny dreams."

Mira thought back to the men who'd come around when her mother was still well. Pale-bodied. Black sunken eyes. Their sick, twisted veins just pulsing in plain view.

Shadow Addicts

The main memory of it was this: Mira hid beneath the bed.

Wild knocks came at the door, and Mira's mother dragged her under the mattress, suspended above them on its frame. Mira sort of tinkered with the box springs. When the door kicked open, she began sobbing.

"We hear you," one of the thieves called. "Best make it easy." They laughed odd-shaped laughter that brought chills to Mira's skin.

Her mother's eyes were red, her face trembling. Hands reached for her beneath the bed. She kicked wildly. "No," she screamed, "go away," she cried, "leave me be."

They grabbed hold of Mira's mother, dragged her from beneath the bed, and she wailed and shrieked, and they beat her legs until she let go of the bed, and pulled her into the yard and Mira ran to the window to see.

Two men held Mira's mother by the wrists, her face toward the sun.

"Relax," said one of the men who then dropped to his knees. He lowered his face to her shadow and began hogging it up.

"No," screamed Mira's mother. "Don't take it all. I feel it," she said. The man on his knees drinking. "Leave me some. Don't make me like that."

When he was done, they dropped her.

"Dammit you were supposed to share," said one of the men who'd held her.

"I'm no good at sharing." And they walked away, the non-sippers grumbling.

Mira's mother searched around. "Mira," she cried out. "Mira."

Once the men were gone, Mira ran outside to her. "There only needs to be a little bit," her mother said. "If they left a bit, I'll be okay. I don't need the whole thing. I'm not like that. It doesn't have to be perfect. It doesn't have to be whole."

They investigated the ground, but there was nothing but light. Wherever she stood, it was as though she wasn't there. Her shadow was gone. It would stay gone forever.

"It's not fair," Mira's mother said. "It's not fair what they've done to me."

Night Hunting Too

But that is far removed from the night when Mira's mother sent her out into the scant moonlight to collect a shadow so she might sleep. Far removed, though it is the cause.

Mira is in the fields.

In the midst of swarms of dark.

The panic and the dim light.

The crescent moon above her, grinning. The stars twinkling, many of them suns with their own planets close by.

Mira flirts with this notion.

On every planet is it the same?

On every world are girls like her hunting shadows for their mothers?

Mira sees a rabbit in the field. It is frozen, its ears aloft like antennae, searching the sounds Mira's steps make. It turns to her, and even from that distance, because she has spent so much of her life with rabbit shade in her mouth, has swallowed some of it into her soul, she can tell the animal: I need your help.

She doesn't do it with language. She doesn't do it with signs. She doesn't know exactly how, but it happens.

"What kind of help?" the rabbit asks.

Mira explains. She needs shadow. For her mother, she needs it.

The rabbit looks up at the moon.

"Will it hurt?"

"Nah," says Mira, "not really."

"Why should I trust you?"

"You ever spoken with someone like me? Has this ever happened?"

"There are plenty of things that happen for the first time," the rabbit says. "There are things that only happen once. Just because it's rare doesn't mean it's special."

"Then ask yourself. Does it seem like I'm lying?"

The rabbit's nose twitches, its whiskers go side to side. "No," it says. "It doesn't."

"Then you'll help?"

"What do we do?"

"First," says Mira, "I need you near me. I can come to you, or you can come here. Whichever you prefer."

"I'll come to you," says the rabbit, and, slowly, it makes its way.

"It won't hurt but you'll never be the same. I'll just take a bit, and I'll never ask you again, but if I accidentally do just say, 'I've helped you before,' and I'll say, 'much obliged,' and you can just go on." Mira keeps still in the night, waiting for the reply to come. The smooth skin of her shoulders aglow with moonlight. The music of night birds warbling all around.

"Okay," the rabbit says, and Mira lowers her head. She takes a mouthful of shadow from the ground in her cheeks. She holds it. Then the rabbit's on its way.

MIRA WALKED THROUGH the field back toward home. But as she moved, she heard a sound. A humming. A tune. A song.

"A world with two suns," she heard, "that is the dream."

Mira walked along.

"What's this?" Murk asked, hobbling up. "Mira, you out turning tricks?"

Mira showed him her middle finger.

"Ah, what's wrong?" Murk tapped her shoulder. "So quiet," he said, then realizing, "Ah. Mouth full of dark? Swallow it. We'll go get in trouble."

Mira pushed him.

"I like 'em rough. What's it you got?"

Mira held two fingers up behind her head.

"Rabbit?" said Murk. "For your mom?"

Mira could only nod.

"Tunnels and burrows and darkness and warmth."

Mira shrugged.

"Was that you at the train today? They sped it up."

Mira moved along, and Murk followed in his limping way.

"Then thanks."

Mira rolled her eyes.

"You should go every day," Murk said. He pointed at her full cheeks, began to sing. "A world with two suns, and both are for me."

Mira spit out the shadow and it evaporated, disappeared. "I've told you that song is bullshit."

"You're talking now?"

"Don't think I want to, but I got a question."

"I've got loads of answer." Murk stretched in the moonlight.

"Loads of shit more like. Hairstyle thief."

Murk kicked dirt at Mira with his peg. "It's from the damn album cover," he said. "I already told you."

"Then that guy's a hairstyle thief."

Murk tucked his hair behind his ears. "He died like a hundred and fifty years ago."

"He could see the future."

"And it's not even done yet. It's gonna be longer. It'll look different when it's done."

"Fine."

"It's gonna be like down to here," Murk motioned a bit below his shoulders. "Ain't a thing about you I wanna be like."

"Whatever," said Mira. "Look, here's the question."

"I don't know I feel like sharing my answer with you anymore."

"Then just share your bullshit. Tell me why you think they're out here."

Murk fingered his hair a bit, "Who?"

"The domers."

"How the hell should I know?"

"Mom thinks they might can fix it. She's heard of people getting well. With leeches and enemas. Crystals or candles. Maybe they've got something like that but better. Something that works for real."

"Then let her think it."

"She wants me to ask."

Murk's black eyes widened, glistened. "How?"

"I'm guessing politely."

"They'll shoot you if you get close enough."

"Didn't today."

Murk puzzled a moment. "They *didn't* shoot today."

"Or yesterday. Or the day before that."

"You've gone all those times?"

"Yep."

"Why?"

"Reasons."

"I wouldn't let 'em fix me if they could."

"You can fix yourself," Mira said. "Keep your shadow on the outside and you'll be just fine."

"I'm fine."

"Cause of that peg."

"A blessing and a curse. What you gonna do now?"

"Maybe ask. I don't know."

"Nah," said Murk. "You lost your momma's rabbit shadow."

"Shit," Mira said.

AFTER MIRA LEFT Murk, she strolled some, looking for whatever she might chance into for a shadow for her mom, fumbling Bale's image in her mind. He hadn't shot her, and he'd been nice enough. She figured, if she asked him, he'd tell her. But she considered then what he'd said. About the names from a hat. Whether or not she had magic. Could she find him again?

She trekked around considering her fate for what she figured was an hour then made her way home.

When she got there, Mira lowered herself to her mother's face, her mother quivering with anticipation. "I stayed gone an hour," Mira said. "Couldn't find a thing."

Her mother cussed a bit, tossed in her chair, was devastated. "It ain't fair," she said, but Mira tried to ignore it.

Captain

Captain Flamsteed barked on at Bale, their faces so close the two traded breath.

"In so many ways your ridiculous indecision has allocated a remarkable risk on the function of our enterprise. We are currently more susceptible to incursions because of your curiosity and ineptitude. It's an odd shadow, son, so be it. Question not the motivations and dictations of your superiors in this regard. We have established protocols with remarkable foresight by looking to past infractions enacted against our intentions." Flamsteed's deep breath, "So, in order to make certain that my dispensation of regulation isn't unmitigated meandering falling on deaf ears, I must demand again that you clarify your intentions should this blinking-shadowed beast show herself again at the outskirt of our camp's circumference."

"I'll shoot," Bale said.

"It is imperative that you do just that. Otherwise, I'll have no choice other than to arrive at the conclusion that you are indeed a sympathizer," he turned his back to Bale, "and I'll be forced to stop the train." Flamsteed circled Bale, walked to Drummond. "Please disclose what transpires if and when the train is stopped."

"Exiled," Drummond said. "Thrown the fuck out."

"Understood?"

"Understood," said Bale.

Mira Returns

She was back and Bale had her in his sights. The train chugged around on its track.

Bale figured he'd give one warning. He raised his bullhorn. "My orders are to shoot."

Mira stopped. It was Bale's voice. She recognized it. And Mira considered his orders. When she'd woken that morning to come to the train, she'd assumed that no matter what, she'd never have to deal with her mother again. If they had a cure, she'd be free. And if she got herself shot . . .

Bale put the crosshairs on her heart. He cleared his throat. He took a breath.

"Sweet shit," he said to himself. But she asked for it.

He had never killed a girl. He had shot a few men. The first two were from close range. Two quick reports from his rifle. One shot had found its victim's face, had entered the head of the man just below the eye—a hole the size of a fingertip—had exited the back of his skull—the hole the size of Bale's fist, a chunk of hair and cranium popped off as debris. The other man got caught in the belly, and he laid up in the grass for a good time bleeding out as the captain asked him questions that he never got good answers to. "Who sent you? Why have you come here?" And the dying man just moaning nonsense, his midnight-colored eyes glaring, his black blood staining his shirt and the grass blades and the earth.

The two men had come up when the train was stalled, while they were off-loading the curved track the train now moved along. It might have even been accidental, their coming. They just strayed up to the train, to their deaths.

Bale hated the look of their lifeless bodies slunk down, maybe hated the sight of their falling even more.

He didn't want to see Mira fall like that.

Bale aimed the rifle where he had to.

Then Bale pulled the trigger.

The Marvelous Murk

Just beyond the train-circled outposts stood Murk—his hair messed, his eyes dark as tar. He buttoned the top snap of his leather jacket, he tightened the rope round his waist.

"A world with two suns," he said.

The train had picked up speed, so now was the time. He raised his crossbow to his shoulder.

"May your aim be sweet and true," he said.

He pulled the trigger.

The arrow launched, dragging rope as it flew.

It struck the train.

Murk reached down and undid a buckle and his wooden leg slipped free and fell to the ground.

The rope grew taut.

Murk ballooned his body, so it expanded like a kite, and then the rope snagged his waist, and he was pitched from the ground in a heave and pulled skyward with vigor, the air crisp on his face as he went aloft.

Up and away he went, into the clouds, his black eyes shining as though an orchestra played just for him.

Into the white clouds, thick the way cake is thick, chill as cold peaches.

When the length of rope went slack, he cut it and spread himself some more, sailed along.

"That is the dream," he sang.

Near him, buzzards circled.

He stuck his tongue out at them, said, "Shit eaters." But really, he owed them so much.

It was those birds he had seen so ridiculously ambulating on the ground but so spiritual in the sky, their black bodies smart against the blue of it. He had watched them, how they hovered, rarely beating their wings, catching currents of wind and rising and falling and twirling and twirling endlessly, and Murk had to try it.

Before the train, he'd had to rely on Mira.

"Faster damn it," he'd scream at her as she pulled the rope to get him going.

"Says the one legger."

"Only on the ground," he'd say. "Up here, I'm immortal."

Sometimes it'd take hours of her pulling to get him flying, but since the train arrived, it had been easy.

It was by accident he'd learned their trick. He had neared the train out of curiosity, and he saw how it gathered speed when people approached, and then they started firing bullets.

"Tomorrow," he told Mira the first time, "you should go and see the train. It's beautiful."

He didn't mention the bullet stuff.

"You should've seen how high I got," Murk told Mira once he'd finally soared back to earth, found his leg and visited her.

"I nearly got killed."

"Nearly counts for nothing though."

"Well, I'm not doing it again." But, of course, she did.

Twice more after much persistence on his part. These past few times, though, were not because of his coaxing.

Why she was going mattered little to Murk. As long as he was able to soar, he was happy. Mira made it possible for him, and because of that, he appreciated her.

"Swallow your shadow and come fly with me," he said to her once.

"I don't have one to swallow."

"Yes you do," he said. "I don't know where you keep it, or how you keep it hidden, but you have one. I can smell it."

"A world with no sun," Mira sang at him, stealing his tune, making it her own. "That is the dream."

BUT NOW IT is Murk, aloft. Coasting. His ballooned self catching the currents and tossing him as a feather might be tossed. Sailing softly as a leaf plucked from the topmost branch of a tree.

Below, there is a gunshot.

Below, another shot.

Murk hears them much later than the shots are fired, as sound travels slowly and he is far away, but, when he hears them, he says a small prayer for Mira, who he imagines is the target, and who might already be dead. He isn't worried enough to land and find out. But when he finally does come down, he goes to her house. Murk would never admit it to her, but if Mira died, it would bother him.

Bale the Sympathizer

Flamsteed asked again, "Please explain to me the nature of what transpired. I'm confused as to what you are suggesting. Simply stated: you missed?"

"Sort of," said Bale. He slouched now, his strong body casual, his hands in his pockets, looking away from Flamsteed.

The captain was frenetic, his voice like electricity. "I feel like I am missing some vital segment of the scenario at hand."

Bale pulled his hands from his pockets, laid them opened and smiled. "You told me to shoot," he told the captain. "So, I shot." Bale figured he was going to be punished, but something in his demeanor suggested he didn't give a fuck.

Murk the Disbeliever

Murk seemed confused. "So? He missed. It's good."

"Sort of," said Mira. She was staring at the spot on the ground where her shadow should be.

Murk was leaned against the wall of Mira's home. He had pulled off his peg leg and was scratching his back with it. "I don't understand," said Murk, his face showing relief, his hands working the peg fiercely. "Why do you seem bothered?"

"Because," said Mira, "I think he only missed on purpose."

Exiled

Every citizen of the outpost was called to the northernmost edge by a single bugle player who blew some sad tune awkwardly so that it slipped from the navel of his brass instrument in handicapped fashion.

The sun was near setting.

The captain shot a flare into the air. It burned orange and dragged across the sky toward the east where dusk sat grayly culminating, the fire of the flare fizzling into smoke that nearly matched its backdrop, and the train slowed.

"I address you now in order that I might impress a profound punishment upon one of your peers," said Flamsteed. Bale stood naked with his hands covering his cock and balls. "Here is a man who holds sympathy for those beyond the train." There was a deepened sense of ceremony in Flamsteed's voice, almost ministerial, and the other outpost dwellers sighed out palpably. Amassed there in their white fatigues, they hung their heads. The women watched Bale's nude body; most of the men stared at the dirt. "This man cannot continue to live on amongst us."

The train's caboose was pulling into view, and just behind it, the only exit from the town, the gap between it and the engine— a sort of circling void.

Drummond seized Bale's arm and walked him forward. A surge of murmurs from the bystanders clucked up as they moved along.

When they came to the track, Drummond whispered, "I tossed a rifle from the northwest tower over the train. If you run, you can get it before they start shooting."

"Run? On this?" Bale balked at the stone-scattered ground in front of his feet.

Drummond turned back toward the captain.

"Yeah, I'll miss you too," Bale said.

Again the bugle player blew his pathetic tune.

Bale stepped lightly onto the mean little rocks on the other side of the track, and his legs tried to lighten themselves and he quivered in his moving.

The train began to huff and chug.

Bale set off. Stumbling and tarrying forward, striding as quickly as he could. Huff and chug, huff and chug.

With each step, his body howled. Stabbing his bare feet into the murderous stones.

He saw the rifle, and a shot was fired.

He kicked harder into the miserable sprint and another shot kicked up dust near the gun.

Bale closed his eyes, dived for the rifle, rolling naked in the rocks, his whole front scraped pink in the fall. He used the gun as a crutch to stand and another shot whizzed by him. All the graying day seemed to swell up with panic. The train was running full. Chugga-chugga. Whee-chugga.

Bale made toward the trees, zigzagging as best he could.

Another shot that nearly got him. He smelled the heat of it clip past his face.

He neared the edge of the white rocks.

Another shot.

The up-ahead grass spat blades.

Another shot.

The dirt coughed dust.

Another shot.

A tree belched splinters.

Another shot.

But nothing.

Bale was into the thicket of trees breathing heavily, somehow safe.

two

The first shadow addict was a young boy from McAlester, Oklahoma, a nowhere city toward the eastern edge of that state, just a few hours' drive from the Ozark Mountains.

His parents had taken him into the hospital for displaying symptoms somewhat like rabies—he tried to bite his father, he chased after passing cars. They'd been out to Robbers Cave, a state park nearby, and assumed maybe he'd been bit by a bat or possum when unattended. Doctors couldn't quite figure it out, especially the blackened eyes, but ultimately they restrained and sedated him, and his symptoms abated. They interviewed the boy, once he was cognizant, but couldn't totally ascertain what might have come over him. "I was just lying in the grass," the boy had said.

When he seemed up for moving about, they took him on a walk to get a feel for his strength, to see if he could be released—the doctors deceiving themselves into believing it was some sort of allergy, some sort of reaction to a thing he ate or drank.

But, when he was again in the sunlight, once they'd taken him outside, the boy dropped to his shadow and gorged it up into himself and went dark again.

News of the condition traveled fast.

The boy was underage and the media couldn't use his real name. They took to calling him Tom Joad, because, at the beginning of The Grapes of Wrath, *Joad is released from a prison in McAlester.*

It was one of those sick accidents the world offers unknowingly.

"I'll be all aroun' in the dark," Tom Joad says at the end of the novel. "I'll be everywhere—wherever you look."

And shadows were everywhere, so nothing could be more true.

Curiosity caught hold of humanity.

"You can't possibly drink a shadow."

Then, of course, they'd have to try.

And the woe of the world was real.

Tom Joad died from experimental procedures in 2029. They enucleated him—took out his eyes—thinking without them some part of the bad magic would come undone. If he couldn't see the sun or moon—or anything at all—wouldn't that help remedy his condition? But it didn't. Still he was ravenous for his shadow. He fought for it, threw himself against windows and struggled against whatever restraint they had him under—his sockets filled with gauze. Even after they lobotomized him, he struggled on. Ultimately, some arsenic-based medicine did him in, the doctors going back to ancient stores once newfangled treatments failed them. By 2030, the world was turning to shit. But a decade danced on, and the sipping spread before the domers took to the domes. Nothing they did helped any. Little wars had broken out and they retreated.

It started like this: The shadow addicts attacked lightbulbs, felled traffic signals and lampposts, neon elements, and beacons. Decimated public arenas and stadiums. Subtracted any source of light that would cheapen the moon's brilliance. The aggressions quickly decimated populations. Across the whole world, cities were thinned.

There was no true governing body, just a kind of mob mentality ensued. Little warlords rose up, were followed by weaker miscreants. Vandals feeding their addictions.

No one knows who figured it first, but the shadow addicts realized other people's shadows worked just as well as their own. And, as their tolerance grew, it seemed necessary to pilfer shade to reach the same highs. They needed more shadow to get fucked up.

Gangs of shadow addicts chased down children on playgrounds, rounded up old ladies from retirement homes, and we've seen what happens to those whose shadows are gone.

Mira and Murk

But you have to know how Mira met Murk. Years ago, she'd found him mutilated, his leg cut away, wailing as though death sat on his chest. Clumped there in thickets of huizaches—brutally thorned midget trees that sprang from the earth like bouquets of bones—he crooned anguish, gabbled desperate nonsense.

Mira'd been out hunting and this was early in that endeavor for her, most likely less than a year after her mother started demanding wild shade. Mira was maybe six then. Maybe seven. She couldn't recall for certain. Murk was around her same age.

Besides nearly dead, he was shadow-wasted, his eyes pitch, skin pale, disease of lust all about him. It was the first time he'd been that way. He drank his shadow just before it could be stolen. It wasn't uncommon. It was better to be a shadow addict than become what Mira's mother was—a beggared version of yourself, dependent on others.

He'd been chased by a group of strange men, had sought refuge amongst the thorny trees, but, upon seeing that their pursuit would not be abated, he lowered himself to the earth and consumed the darkness that fell from his form.

So, they hacked off his leg.

They dragged him from the huizaches as much as he'd allow—his small hands doing their best to cling to the branches he hid amongst—and when Mira found him, Murk's hands were pierced clear through by thorns, sticky with blood.

She'd seen plenty of lack-limbed men and women, ambulating sickly through far-off fields as she hid herself behind the shrunken trees of the landscape.

Stories had been told.

She'd heard, though had never seen to prove it, that some device existed which, through science or magic, extended the life of these limbs, and that they dangled, removed from their owners but not dead and not rotting, in the sunshine to produce human shade to be consumed for a fee.

There must have been a hellish quality to it—some condition of the machine that kept the limbs animate—which granted the dismembered elements the ability to regenerate darkness. Mira had taken from enough animals to know that, once sipped away, the darkness was gone forever. She had come across the same rabbit twice. She'd seen how in the sunlight their shadows were less dark than her own, paler because they'd been skimmed from. But Mira also understood that nothing about the world was absolute.

When she found him, Murk was dying and deranged, the hackled meat of his absent leg perched upon by dozens of mad-buzzing flies.

He tried biting Mira as she plucked his hands from the thorns.

She'd never be able to entirely understand why she helped, why she took him home and treated him. Poured salt water on his hands. Lit a fire and cauterized his leg—her mother telling her how but not helping—wrapped his wounds with herbs and gauze. Let him lay near death on the floor of her home, and she wasn't entirely certain he remembered all the good she'd done for him. It rarely came up in conversation, and he had never truly thanked her.

When she was sure he'd live, she'd dragged him back to the thorns where she'd found him. For all she knew, he thought it was a bad dream, a sort of festering nightmare that he'd woken butchered and flubbed by.

But they'd remained in some way linked. They seemed drawn to each other in the wilderness. He had a way of finding her, of earning her aid. She had flown him like a kite. She had dodged bullets for him that first time he sent her to the train. She had no idea why. He would ask some preposterous thing, and she'd oblige him. She'd listen to his rants. She'd tolerate his abuses. But she never told him the secrets of her own. Where she put her shadow, how she hid it. How she could sleep on her own even without one. And that stupid song he sang . . .

"It doesn't work," said Mira.

"What?" Murk would be singing, his black eyes transfixed as though performing for an imaginary crowd. His hips wagging in a sort of one-legged sex way.

"Your song?"

"Why not?" He'd go still.

"Two suns would make two weaker shadows. That's all."

"So . . ."

"So it'd be the same as having one single shadow," Mira said, her brown eyes riled as though she were saying some impossibly simple thing. "If anything, sing for a brighter sun."

Murk mimed a strangling gesture. "Sometimes," he said, "I just can't fucking stand you."

Mira thought the same thing.

THE EVENING THE train was stopped and Bale cast out, Mira and Murk were together. They'd gone back to the train to contemplate it in tandem. There was no certain objective to this mission. They moved amongst the thorny trees, their clothes catching against the snagging limbs, watching the train's circling with squinted eyes. Cicadas grumbled their quasi-mechanical static. A fluorescent hiss of a mating song. The lusty scent of mesquite sap dribbling.

When the train's brake was thrown, and the shrieking halt ensued, the two waited curiously.

"Ever seen 'em do that?" asked Mira.

"Nope."

They waited, watching.

Quickly, Murk got bored. To pass the time, he snapped his fingers. If you did it right, it'd make the male cicadas come close. He liked pulling off their wings.

There was an emptied-out cicada chrysalis on the tree trunk Mira leaned on. She plucked it off—its sticky legs and broke-open bulbous eyes. As Murk contemplated his snapping, glared around for coming bugs, Mira perched the thing in his locks, said, "There's something in your hair."

Murk reached absently with his non-snapping hand, geeked

out a bit when his fingers touched the discarded exoskeleton, said, "Meh," and pawed at the thing like a spaz, stepping away until the crunchy remains were in his fingers. "Hilarious," he said to Mira, and she was chuckling, and then they heard the bugle.

"Is that music?" Mira asked.

The train had stopped in such a position that Mira and Murk could see those gathered beyond.

"Kind of," said Murk.

"Better than that song you're always singing."

Murk poked Mira's ribs.

She was close enough to see her reflection in his blackened-out eyes.

In the distance, someone stepped across the tracks.

Murk tucked his messed hair behind his ears. "That boy's naked," he said. "And he's running."

About that time, they started firing shots. The white rocks kicked dust. The bang-bangs of more gun blasts rang out and the naked guy picked up speed. The runner rolled, rose, and turned toward the trees.

Bale in Exile

Bale sat naked, his back to a mesquite trunk, huffing breath. The limbs of the thing draped down toward the ground, bends of them rested on the dirt. It was as though the tree was a bark-covered hand, roosted on its fingertips. The thumb was the trunk, the limbs the other fingers. Above, the canopy he took cover under, somehow the palm of the thing. He'd never been beneath a tree. He lounged in awe of it. He heard a few more shots. He inspected the rifle, ejected the magazine, counted the rounds. He'd half expected Drummond to leave a single bullet, a way out if he chose it, but his big brother had loaded up. Bale had fifteen shots. His feet ached, he had scrapes down his front, and he had to find food, water, and shelter. The wasteland of his life to come was, at that time, unimaginable. It'd be like trying to consider where you stand in relation to the universe while a house you're trapped in is on fire. His balls dipped in the dirt. He could feel grass blades in his ass crack.

Mira, Murk, and Bale

From where she was, Mira could see it was Bale. She and Murk were hidden from his view. They had split up, she and Murk. They lurked behind trees, fully camouflaged.

"Why'd you leave the train?" she asked.

Bale aimed toward her. "Mira?"

"I came out to ask you something. Yesterday. You shot. You missed. That why?"

"I missed on purpose," said Bale. "And, yeah, I guess partly."

Mira paused to think it through. She picked an acorn from the ground. She was beneath a live oak, and acorns were scattered everywhere, dropping from the branches every minute or so. Bale had his gun. Murk camped where he was. Mira was thinking.

If you've never seen an acorn, it has two main parts—the cupule and the nut. The cupule's like a little hat, designed to fall away from the hard shell that covers the fruit, and Mira picked this off, set it on the tip of her pinky, wagged the finger like a little performer with a cap on. She contemplated the naked nut then, rolled it in the palm of her other hand. She took the cupule from her pinky, seated it back on the nut. She took it off. Set it back again. "Murk," she hollered, but Murk didn't answer. "Murk," she hollered again.

"What?"

"Throw him your jacket."

BALE FELT BETTER in the jacket, but his feet still throbbed. He had Mira's canteen, and if he raised it too high, his naked parts showed. Mira turned away and Murk snickered a bit as the stream of water running from the canteen slowed, and Bale held his tongue out as the last beads of water dropped.

"I know the feeling," said Murk, but Bale thinned his eyes, lowered the canteen, didn't understand him.

"They made you leave?" Mira asked.

"Yeah." Bale tried to drink again from the drained canteen. The thing huffed emptily when he pulled it from his lips. He checked the ground around her, "Because . . ." but, in his investigating, he could not find Mira's shadow. "It's gone again?"

Murk laughed, "She never shows it. Keeps it hid."

"Back there she had one that could turn off and on. Only one like it I ever saw."

"She what?" Even black-eyed bastards get their feelings hurt some, and if you were there you would have felt the air go weird.

No one spoke. A kiskadee called its steady, trill peal. Acorns dropped. Ground skinks flittered through loose leaves and debris.

Bale must have felt the mood drift a bad way. He threw Mira her canteen back.

Bale's eyes moved from Mira to Murk, Murk to Mira.

He considered their hair.

"I got the same haircut as my brother too," he said. "All the guys in the dome do. No choice to it. Girls have different hair-cuts. I mean, they all have the same haircut, but it's different from the boys." Bale kind of touched his head as he talked and Murk closed his eyes.

"I'm growing it out," Murk said. "It's gonna be to here," he said, rubbing his fingers just below his shoulders. He wore a gray T-shirt that was half eaten by moths, cotton so thin you could see his nipples straight through it.

"He thinks you're my brother."

"You're not?" said Bale.

"God no," said Mira. "I'd have to kill myself."

"Guys in the other train town had different hair," Murk said. "Long on top and combed over. Shaved on the sides. I had mine a bit like that when I was younger. Mira would cut it for me. She's got clippers. Remember?"

"Unfortunately."

"Other train town?" said Bale.

Murk gained his bearings. "Yeah, there's a few. One east of here."

"How far?"

"Half day's walk, I guess."

"Can you show me?" It was really just a nervous question Bale asked, but once it was said aloud, he felt he had to justify his asking it. "I know there's other domes. Didn't realize they were sending out trains too."

"I'll think about it."

It was quiet then. Bale's toes were bleeding.

Drummond Left Behind

Drummond breathed deep the calming outdoor air. He raised his binoculars, scoured the countryside, saw nothing of consequence. When he climbed down from the tower, Flamsteed was there.

"You know we have to detain you. It's only for a short time," Flamsteed said.

Drummond stared into the captain's eyes.

DRUMMOND AND FLAMSTEED entered a car of the train, followed by three others. Most of the train was empty. The captain and a few other superiors kept quarters there. The engineers who operated the train lived aboard. And there were holding cells. They made their way down a corridor to one of these. The captain spun a wheel on the cell door's front and Drummond heard a lock release. The door was eased open, sang rustily, and Flamsteed said, "I'm going to have to search your person. For your own safety."

The cell was dark, rust scented. "For my safety?"

"Under periods of isolation suicidal ideation is common and

if you have a weapon, or some semblance of weaponry, your thoughts might chance into dark terrain."

Drummond raised his hands over his head in anticipation of a pat down.

The captain frowned. "I'm afraid that won't be sufficient."

Drummond was puzzled.

"Your clothes," said the captain. "I'll need you to disrobe."

DRUMMOND STEPPED NAKED into the dark, dank room. He heard the captain clank the door closed behind him, heard the lock spin, heard it catch a metallic latch and the click of it echoed in the darkness.

He slouched in the gloom, sagged to the ground. After a while, the train began to move.

In the dark, Drummond's mind twisted visions from imagined colors. He watched with eyes open in the stark, shuttered-off world as figments of Bale knelt beneath a mesquite tree, toyed with his rifle.

He checked the walls around him. They were steadfast. He jumped for the ceiling but couldn't touch it.

There was no way out. He knew. He knew before he started. The investigation was futile but he needed to assure his mind.

Ghastly

Bale fantasized his surroundings were some kind of make-believe. Foreign images. Newfangled smells. Nothing triggered memory. Moving on aching, bare feet behind Murk and Mira, he wondered if his new acquaintances would feel as overwhelmed in the dome. But he decided it wouldn't be the same. They'd feel confined. Why wasn't the opposite true for him? He didn't feel free, let out of a cage. He felt weighted down by the vastness of it all.

"Where we going?"

"To Mira's," Murk said.

"We'll get you dressed there. In my father's old clothes. Need to rest a minute?"

Bale's green eyes shocked in their sockets. "No," he said. "Just wish I had shoes."

On they moved, through odors foreign to Bale. Sweet and damp. Clean and heavy.

In the distance, the sun was halved by the horizon. The light of the world went orange, became laced with the dark outlines of tree limbs. Birds sang their clucking language. Insects chirped and jingled tunes.

"We don't have far to go," said Mira. Then, "Just through those trees."

"Should you bring anything back?" Murk asked. "For your mom?"

"Probably. Keep an eye out."

"There's a green jay, on that branch there."

"I hate taking from small birds."

It seemed Bale was listening to alien language.

"Under the conditions," said Murk, "don't think you should be picky. We can't really take our half-naked friend here hunting the countryside."

Mira knelt to dirt, watched the bird shadow dance with the mild breeze. She traced the tree-cast darkness on the ground, zeroed in on the bird's shape. "Sorry," she said toward it, then, carefully, she sipped up a bit, changing the darkness just before it disappeared, the bird, having felt the molestation, leaving its perch by batting its wings, taking to the sky.

"What was that?" asked Bale, but Mira, whose cheeks were now slightly bulging, only shook her head and they moved forward. "What'd you do?" Bale asked again.

"Just watch," said Murk, and the three moved on into the mesquite forest that housed Mira's home.

There, they followed Mira to the porch where her mother sat, pale. Her eyes oddly tired, her countenance jittery. Ghastly, you might've called her.

"Evening," Murk said to her, and the woman replied a kind of nonsensical utterance.

Mira lowered her face to her mother's. The two touched

lips. The woman fell to sleep instantly, her tiny face aiming off at nothing as her head slumped toward her shoulder. "Shade trading," Mira said. "I guess that's what you'd call it. Her shadow was stolen. She can't sleep without it."

Bale's pretty teeth in Bale's hung-open mouth.

MIRA DID THE best she could, but her father was smaller than Bale. She rummaged drawers, rooted through closets. In the end, Bale wore a dark denim shirt, pants of the same material and boots of brown leather with yellow nylon strings. A laborer's kind of uniform, it seemed to him. Sleeve cuffs at his forearms. Pant hems at his calves.

"How's it feel?" Mira asked.

"Like I'm wearing someone else's clothes." He seemed a goat in an outfit for house cats. "Snug but whatever." Mira had also found him sleeping things. Shorts too small for him. A ratty kind of V-neck that barely reached his hips. Bale hoisted these clothes. "I'll wear these others for now," and he made his way back to a bathroom he employed as his changing station. It was Mira's, the bathroom. Girl colors and pretty smells. Bale had to fight the urge to hunt around. He didn't know what he'd look for, exactly, but it seemed such a personal space that there had to be good secrets there.

The sleeping clothes were maybe even snugger. When he went back to the heart of the house, Murk was seated in a shabby recliner.

"Hey, hey," Murk said, and motioned with his finger for Bale to do a twirl, but Bale didn't. "So we're not going tonight?" said Murk. He had taken off his leg and sort of cradled it across his chest.

"Going?" said Bale.

"See the other train, if you still want to."

Bale had forgotten. "I do," he made some unintelligible gesture, "but, yeah, I'm tired anyhow." He didn't know where to sit.
Nervousness kept his mouth running. "Just wanna know what
they're like. Back home, we'd talk about the other domes. They
were numbered. Well, numbered and lettered. I was in B3.
Always said that A9 had the prettiest girls, C2 was supposed to
be nothing but deaf folks. Don't know if any of that's true. Don't
know where all that came from. I just kind of wanna see, y'know,
what they wear, I guess."

It was silent a minute and then Mira came in. "Hungry?" she
asked Bale.

"Starving."

Mira moved toward the kitchen, spoke over her shoulder at
him. "We got eggs. I can fry some up."

"Eggs?"

"Yeah. Chicken eggs. You like 'em?"

"Never had 'em."

"Wait," said Murk. "What do y'all eat back there?"

"Rations. Until the crops come in. We've got stuff planted,
but I don't know what. We've all got jobs and mine's not
farming."

"Rations?"

"It's like," Bale said, touching his little shirt, his shorts. "I don't
know what to compare it to. It's food."

"What's it made of?" Mira asked.

"Dunno."

"Is it vegetables? Grain?" said Murk.

Bale felt stupid. "Guess I never really asked."

"I'll make eggs," said Mira. "And we got milk."

"Milk? Like for babies?"

"Yeah," said Murk. "Like for babies. You're gonna suck on Mira's titties."

"Shut up, Murk," Mira said. Then, "From goats."

"Goats make milk?"

"The brown ones make chocolate milk," said Murk, laughing, his leg clutched tight in his hands. His eyes sloe—like deep holes in his head.

"Shut the fuck up," said Mira. "C'mon." She led Bale to the table in the kitchen.

To ANYONE FAMILIAR with one, the egg is a mundane thing, but, if foreign to you, the thing is a miracle. It exists in its own packaging—viscous when raw, solid when cooked. Bale watched Mira crack three into a bowl, and he wasn't sure if the things were alive before their brown shells were broken. He thought, perhaps, their casings were exoskeletons and what landed in the bowl were organs or innards. A terrible student while in the dome, he'd a vague recollection of what these things were, but, as he watched, he confused them in some way with caterpillars, thinking, as Mira cooked, that what she'd done with the egg was to extract an animal from its chrysalis, disturbing the cycle wherein the goop of the egg was to morph into the bird it would be. But he didn't dwell on these thoughts long.

Mira dropped a pat of butter into the pan on the stove, and the smell of it caramelizing radiated through the kitchen, made Bale's stomach ache in a way it never had. Until then, everything he'd eaten was of some secretive manufacture, a kind of paste the color of tree bark that tasted consistently of nothing but nutrition—a food made from a formula rather than a recipe.

Mira handed him a glass of goat's milk—a new mystery. He took a small sip from the glass, then gulped away. It was wholesomely perverted. It was shamefully gratifying.

Bale listened then as Mira poured the whisked eggs into the pan, heard them hiss as they hit, and watched Mira work them with a wooden spoon briefly before leaving her spot at the stove—watched her lean form, her hips. She set a plate and fork in front of Bale. Smiled so soft at him Bale thought he might giggle. Her eyes seemed to know things. Some brief silences have a thousand years inside them. She stepped away, an energy retreating with her, came back a moment later with the pan of eggs in her hand. She scraped them onto the plate.

"Eat up," Mira said. Then, noticing a kind of shock in Bale, said, "Something wrong?"

Bale shook his head. "No. Just didn't think they'd be this color."

Murk and Bale
Talk Shadows

That next morning, Mira's mother woke screaming. A discord ensued. Bale, who'd slept on the sofa, under a quilt made from slapdash-selected fabrics, was perplexed at the chaos of it. Murk hopped alive, pegless out of the recliner, wearing only boxer shorts, rubbing his stump. Mira emerged from a back bedroom to tend to her mom. Things fumbled about. Human smells hovered. Murk turned on music, bobbed his head to it.

"I love mornings," he said toward Bale. "The sun comes up." He shook his hair.

In Bale's world, all things had been scheduled. People moved in straight lines to meet itineraries. This new disorder was bewildering. He thought a moment. He had nowhere to be. The speakers bleated tunes. "How do y'all have electricity?"

Mira, who intercepted the question passing through, said, "Solar panels on the roof." She wore a cotton robe that stopped at her thighs. She touched the hem of the robe. "About like you yesterday in Murk's jacket." She went to the kitchen, banged around a bit. Pots and pans. Tea kettle. "I won't be able to leave her like this."

"Just you and me then," Murk said. "Bring your gun. We'll shoot shit." Murk killed the music, began getting dressed.

"Only got fifteen rounds." Bale gathered up Mira's father's clothes to change into.

"We'll only shoot fifteen things."

"Don't shoot anything you don't have to," Mira called from the kitchen. "If it were up to Murk you'd waste all your bullets on tree stumps and jackalopes."

"What's a jackalope?" Bale asked.

"A thing that ain't real," Mira said.

WHEN THEY SET off, Bale asked, "How long will we be gone?"

"Back by night," Murk told him.

They headed out into the thicket, walked cautiously through the thorny limbs until they came to an open grassland that Murk hopped into—he seemed a scarecrow gifted with life. He found the sun and put his back to it, lowered himself to the thin shadow that had leached from him and gulped it up, began singing, "A world with two suns." He rolled to his back, looking pleased at the sky. But, once propped up on his elbows, he saw Bale kneeled, his rifle shouldered, the barrel of the thing aimed at Murk's heart.

"Your eyes," said Bale, "they're black as fuck."

"Thank God. It still works. I always worry. You know, you're real fucking big. I bet your shadow would fuck me up." A thin, puzzling laughter stretched from him. Murk's head disfigured a bit, quivering. Hallucinatory.

"What now?"

"We go to the train."

"But your eyes. When they're like that. They tell us it makes you evil. Can I trust you? You gonna try to do stupid shit?"

"I might do stupid shit, but you can trust me." Murk pulled up at his trouser leg. His wood peg showed. "There's not enough of me." He stood sloppily, his balance wobbled. "I mean, I could drink up other shadows and get darker, I guess. Like your shadow. But I'm not so lost as that. Look at my wrist." There was some kind of serial number tattooed there. On his other wrist as well. Murk raised his pant leg revealing his ankle. The number was there too. "Somewhere," said Murk, "there's another leg with the same marking. I've never looked for it, but maybe someday I'll find it. It's being gone makes me less dark, but because it's gone is the reason I get dark at all. If I had a whole one like you? All big and shit? If I drank it, I'd be a shitty mess, I guess. Folks with full shadows? They're peculiar *and* mean. Me? I'm just peculiar."

"Find the other leg?"

Murk rambled toward the train they were after. "Sure, it's why they're tattooed. My mom did it. So I could try to track 'em down if they were stole. I don't know what she was thinking there. She used to pray to some God who told her to do it. There's a place they get taken to, the legs. The arms. Shadow addicts like to cut on folks."

"A place they get taken to?"

"That's what I'm told."

THEY MARCHED ON in the humid morning air, their shoes slick with dew and their shirts moist with sweat. Thorns littered the grass and the parched dirt lay dry-cracked and scraggy.

"How old do you think I am?" Murk asked.

"Don't know?" said Bale. "How old?"

"It was an honest question. Your guess is as good as mine. You like flying?"

"Flying? Never have."

"I'm not an idiot," said Murk. "You're a domer. You may as well have spent your whole life in a coffin or beneath a canoe. I'm asking if you like the concept."

"The concept?"

"See that bird up there? Does it do anything for you?"

Some black bird listed across the sky. "I'm not sure."

"Then it doesn't. You'd know right off if it did."

They jostled as they moved over the craggy land. "I've not seen all that many birds," said Bale.

"What'd you do for fun?"

"Fun?"

"In the dome? To pass the time?"

"Worked," Bale said, "or avoided working. Slept. Went to school. Watched the girls shower."

"I like to fly," said Murk. "You have any rope?"

Bale touched a shirt pocket. "I don't . . ."

"Of course not," said Murk. "Why would you? But I have a few yards. Feel like running?"

Bale stopped and Murk walked some distance before realizing. Once he did, he turned toward his slack-stepped acquaintance.

"What the fuck are you talking about?" Bale asked.

"Running," he said, and Murk mimed the practice.

"I know what running is."

"Then why'd you ask?"

"Listen: flying, fun, rope, running? I'm not following you at all. The shadows make you silly?"

"Yes," said Murk. "Very silly. But what does that have to do with it?"

Bale stretched in his tight clothes, trying to make them bigger, fit better.

Murk reached into his jacket and produced a length of rope. "I tie it round my waist. You run. Pull it."

"What the fuck?" said Bale.

"You've already asked that," said Murk. "And now I'm telling you," he said. "I'm telling you what the fuck." Then, slowly, "I TIE THIS," he motioned to the rope, "ROUND MY WAIST," he motioned to his waist, "YOU RUN," he mimed running. "PULL IT." He tugged toward the sky. "No reason we should both be stuck on the ground."

"I don't understand."

"Of course you don't." Murk's gray grin. "You're a domer," he said. "Might as well've spent your whole life in my pocket or up a jackalope's ass." He began to tie the rope around his waist. "A world with two suns," he said, "that is the dream."

Attack

Drummond's eyes opened. He'd been asleep. In that dim space, he'd nearly forgotten his fate. He breathed slowly, puzzling the darkness, recollecting events. He felt a kind of shame a moment. His nude body seemed gruesome to him. Rust dust clung to his nakedness. He lolled a bit and then he knew: the train had gained speed. He sat alert, listening intently for some sound of coming aggression. It came.

A noise so loud Drummond's eyes saw light erupt—a white, hideous resonance thrummed the dark alive—and Drummond pitched from the surface of the floor, smacked the wall and dragged down it. His face gushed warm blood against his flailed-open palms. The smell of pain. Shock swept his heart. His pulse rattled. The train's wheels screeched and blatted. Outside, gun-shots cracked and popped along. Murder music beating rhythmic. The darkness darkened. His thoughts constricted. Involuntarily, he went. Into the inner cavern of bewilderment.

Faint seized him.

Drummond surrendered to dream.

Flying

"Faster!" Murk—ballooned into his thinner form, organized, as best he could organize himself, like a kite. Beneath him, Bale ran: the rope in his right hand, Murk's peg leg in the other, the butt of the back-strapped rifle slapping his ass. "As fast as you can."

"This is," screamed Bale, hopping grass clots and snag gaps, "as fast as I can."

"It's gotta be faster."

"Love to see you," Bale huffed breath, "try it." His bruised feet throbbed.

"Impossible. I only have one leg." He spread his arms.

"Exactly," said Bale. "And my feet are fucked."

"Let out."

"What?"

"As much rope as you have."

Bale loosened his grip, felt Murk catching the wind and felt the burn of the rope skating against the pad of his hand. "It hurts like hell," he said.

"Slow down," said Murk.

"It hurts."

"Slow," yelled Murk, "down."

Bale secured the rope to stop the burning and stumbled to a walk. He gasped, his shoulders heaving.

"Success. You're better than Mira." Kiting, kiting. Murk aloft. Bale walked backwards, marveling at Murk's flight.

"Train's that way." Murk spit in the breeze. "About an hour more."

EVEN FROM A mile off it looked blundered. The harsh smell of rust and smoke stained the air, and juries of buzzards circled in the distant sky. Some stench of putrescence found them and Murk came down scuffing the earth, dry heaving, his eyes bulging as he hacked. Some grand decay crossed the air like filthy cobwebs. Bitter lace. Rotten beach sand. Murk retched. A thread of sputum dangled from his bottom lip. He coughed and it quivered. He cuffed his hand through it and flung it away toward some grass. It caught on a long blade of it, smeared down like a slug. "You don't smell that?"

"Beginning to. Must be thicker up there."

Murk hid the mask of his face in the collar of his leather jacket. His voice came muffled. "Worst odor ever."

"We should hear it moving by now."

"They never stop it?"

"Only when they're kicking us out."

Bale helped Murk up, and Murk leaned on Bale as he reattached his peg. They walked on cautiously, the foul reek constricting as they advanced. Bale coughed a bit. Murk did the same.

Once close enough, they saw odd graffiti on the cars of the train—black skulls with hashtag eyes.

"Know what it means?" Bale asked.

"Nope. Never seen it but can't be a good thing."

They went quietly to the track's edge, slipped beneath two buckled-up cars, gnarled steel and shredded lumber. The battered outpost within—burnt buildings and toppled towers. In the wreckage, dead bodies strewn, carcasses of fetid flesh mulled upon by carrion crows that dawdled unfazed, their gory beaks thick with congealed blood. Flies tap-tapped against the bloated bodies, the constant buzz of their tiny wings.

"Who did it?" said Bale.

Murk used his jacket like a mask, lowered the thing to answer. "Probably Santa Claus." He hid his face again.

"That like a gang?"

Murk's eyes swelled. He let his jacket collar fall. "Serious? Y'all don't got Santa?"

"Who?"

"Comes down the chimney? Brings presents? For Christmas?" The buzzing. The stench. On occasion some buzzard alighted or disembarked. Claws on the rot or wings against the air. Their wicked-upped eyes like yellow jewels of insanity.

Bale shook his head.

"What about the Easter Bunny?"

Bale was blank.

"Tooth Fairy?"

Blank.

"St. Valentine's?"

"I don't know."

"You got any holidays at all?"

"Holidays?"

"Sweet God," said Murk. He sang, "Jingle Bells, Jingle Bells, Jingle all the way!" Then, "You ain't never heard that?" He dry heaved, nauseous from the death essence. Raised his jacket collar.

"We should see if there's anything worth taking."

"No, no, no," said Murk, his voice muffled. "Presents," he said. He dropped the collar. "Y'all got presents?"

"Like gifts?" said Bale. "Yeah."

"When do you give them? When are they exchanged?" Murk's face hid again.

Bale held up a finger. "On birthdays." He held out another finger, "on Dome Day."

"Dome Day?" Muffled.

"Yeah. Celebrates the day we moved into the dome."

Murk shook his head, put his face out near Bale's. "Why would you celebrate moving to a place with no sun and no Santa?"

THEY CLIMBED IN and out of burnt-open cars, poked at the dead with sticks, looked under debris, came up empty. All about them buzzards dawdled with grim treasures of purloined flesh jiggling from their beaks. Their claws click-clacking.

"Check that one's pockets," said Bale. There was a man perched in ash, half his face burnt back to skull, the other half shiny with decay, smeared with buzzard shit. They scrutinized the mess of it.

"I can't touch him," said Murk. Sunlight twinkled off a bead of plasma that dribbled down the dead man's cheek. A glinting spec of mephitic wetness. The spot where his eyes should be, desiccated and gray.

"He might be where all the smell is coming from," said Bale.

The dead man seemed like an exhibit in a museum of night-mares. A cadaver designed to scar the emotions of spectators.

But then Bale flung forward, skidded to the ground, his face at the dead man's half-rotten skull. Screamed, "The fuck. The fuck."

Because some thief—ash across his brow and whisper-thin hair, clothes tattered and hackneyed—gulped up a swallow of Bale's shadow as they were hypnotized by the decomposition. Bale winced at the death he landed near, and the stranger popped up, sprinted toward the train, ducked beneath one of the cars and was out of view.

Drummond's Deeper Prison

Drummond woke and the train was still. He made to his feet before realizing the train car he was captured in had been toppled. He stood on the wall of the thing, stared at the floor. In whatever incursion that transpired, the sheet metal ceiling was gashed, and a column of light screamed into the otherwise darkness. It seemed unnaturally bright, and Drummond crept to eye the opening, to witness the goings-on of the attack's aftermath.

He saw only wreckage and char, destruction and gore.

Dead bodies lay strewn amongst piles of debris. Threads of smoke bled from mounds of ash.

A cataleptic hush drenched the disorder. A gray apocalypse of whist.

Drummond smelled gunpowder and death. His skin grew goose bumps at the mystery.

Naked, in the dim light, he considered his fate, inspected his soreness.

"Shit," he said to himself, his voice echoing in that metallic space.

His imprisonment was supposed to be a week long. Now, he had no idea. He sat near the sunlight, let the warmth touch his skin.

The Thief

Murk hoisted Bale away from the dead man and they gave chase, ducking the same train car the thief had disappeared beneath, following him out into the field beyond, toward a brush sparsely leaved. Bale shouldered his rifle and thought of firing, but he wasn't certain he could aim for gagging. He figured he'd miss as the thief distanced. His mind filled with the rotting face. The sparkling decay of it. The dead man's skull like twinkling garbage.

Murk grabbed him by the elbow, dragged him on, and the two slowed as they entered a mess of thorny limbs, bobbing into the mayhem of shrubbery.

"Where'd you go?" Murk called out.

They heard tussling.

Rounding an oak tree, they saw the thief cradling an old man who slept in his lap. The man raised a finger to his lips, shushing Bale and Murk. He whispered, "He ain't slept in days."

Bale whispered back, "I don't give a shit 'bout him," and he aimed at the thief, placed the barrel of his rifle against his fore-head, about made to fire a round through his brain.

"Then why you whispering?" The thief seemed affable there—in his dingy attire, in his compromised position. "Name's Jessup," he hissed. "This my pa, Rondell. He's in a bad way."

"Shadow stolen?" said Murk, and Bale's face showed disbelieving.

"Yup." It was like Jessup's voice was made of breeze. He looked like he'd clean a toilet with his bare hands for a sandwich.

Murk leaned on his good leg.

"I'm not about to just let this go without some kind of apology," said Bale. He applied pressure, the barrel driving Jessup's head back and Jessup's eyes thinning with fear.

"Course not, son. If it weren't for desperate measures . . ." he chanced some amenable gesture. "Dad and I are in pursuit, I suppose. He's been aching for sleep. About delirious. We've spent the past three days trailing his thief. We're away from our livestock."

"Livestock?" said Murk.

"We got goats at home. He gets swallows off 'em. Sleeps like a baby. But out here you gotta chase critters, and it ain't all that easy. I lucked into you."

"After his thief?" said Murk. "Why?"

Rondell snored a bit in Jessup's lap. "He passed through our parts. Through here. He's the one that paints them skulls with the tic-tac-toe eyes."

"He sacked the outpost?" said Bale. More pressure from the barrel. Jessup in pain from the pressing, his neck cricked.

"Hell no. Fella's a nothing. A little redheaded troll. Bout chest high to you. Runs alone as far as I know. Snuck up on dad while he napped on the lawn. He'd been drinking. He's a drinker. We both are really. I don't suppose you got any booze?"

"No," said Bale.

"Makes sense." Jessup frowned down at his father. "Whatever got this town was something else entirely. I've seen others the same."

"If your dad's happy back home, why go out after him? Seems too risky just for payback," Murk said.

"Would be, but it's more than just that. We kill him, Dad goes back normal. Well, normal as he used to be." Bale eased a bit. Jessup said, "Dad's healer said so. We went to her straight away when he got like this. She's the one gave us the goats. We did that a few days until he was well enough to set out. We brought one with us but he died of tired a few days back."

"What?" More pressure.

"Yeah, the tired got him. Poor little thing. I don't think we could've taught him to drink shadows. We ate him. He tasted fine."

"The healer part," said Bale.

"Oh, she's never steered Dad wrong yet. Burns off his warts and all. Said there's a comet coming."

"A comet?" said Bale.

"Halley's. Showed it to us in a telescope. You can't see it now, but it's out there. It's gonna bring back shadows. But your thief's gotta die first. She seen it in her science."

The wind pushed tree branches. Birds chirped and cooed.

"You mean like a shooting star?" said Murk. "For wishing with?"

"Bigger. Brighter. Like a tiny sun."

Bale looked at the heavens. Bizarrely broad to him. Almost made his head ache just looking up. "When?"

"A week, maybe. Maybe sooner." Jessup pawed at his clothes, pulled his face away from Bale's barrel. A red circle imprint stained his forehead. He kneaded it with a knuckle. "We set out ill equipped on account of our haste. Did I already ask y'all about booze?"

Bale, lost in his contemplation of the sky, let his rifle barrel ease toward the ground.

"But what's it do to fix anything?" said Murk.

"She had a chart, but I didn't get it. She took away Dad's pneumonia once with an egg."

"An eating egg?" said Bale, his attention back on Jessup.

"Pulled his sick into the egg and cracked it open and the yolk was red and he was better."

"You people are fucked up," said Bale.

Rondell's sleepy breathing rasped.

"Well," said Murk, "I guess good luck."

"Wait," said Bale. "That's it? We're not gonna do anything for payback? Fuckers stole my shadow some."

Murk shrugged. "I mean, seems they're in a bad enough way. But shoot 'em if you want."

Murk had a point. They sat so stranded. So foolish. "Shit," Bale said. "You'll just owe me."

Drummond and the Light

Drummond watched the thin daylight dwindle. The hole in the train car roof faced west. He could see the sunset. The final glint that sat on the horizon glowed like magic. Its orange fire seemed impossible. Its surface subtracted continually as Drummond pressed his face against the metal prison. He seemed locked that way, watching as it disappeared. Hoping something good would come.

Return to Mira

The day dampened. Dusk was up. Murk and Bale worked toward Mira's house. Bale's feet dragged, he'd unbuttoned his shirt, let the breeze sweep over him. Murk hummed, held his jacket folded over an arm.

"Mira have goats?" Bale asked.

"And chickens. And rabbits. Her mom's against it. For whatever reason. Would rather have Mira running all over finding wild shade for her."

"She just a shitty person?"

Murk tucked his hair behind an ear. "Just sick, I guess. You ever hear the Doors?"

"This like flying?"

"Nah. It's a band. Music."

"Nope. They good?"

"Don't tell Mira, but I don't know. I found an album cover of theirs once, but there wasn't a record inside. I liked the guy's hair though. On the cover." Murk picked at a scratch on his jacket. A place the leather was rough.

Cicadas chirped. Birds warbled.

"Think Jessup's right? About murder and the comet."

"There's gotta be something that works, but who knows?"

"Should we tell Mira?"

Murk stopped. "It's a new moon tonight."

"Okay."

"So I'm gonna leave you here. Mira's house is just through there. I don't like anyone to watch me when I'm draining. I'll come tomorrow."

"Draining?"

"No moonlight or sunlight. The darkness drains out all the way. Leaks off and I can't do nothing to stop it for hours. Aches like rust on your bones." Murk seemed afraid. Jittery. His black eyes strained as though he'd cry ink-like tears.

"I get it," Bale said, but he didn't. He almost reached to pat Murk's shoulder but stopped short. "Just through there?" He said, tensing toward Mira's.

Murk twitched. "Not far at all." He paced out into the darkening day, and Bale dipped and bobbed through the branches.

Over Soup

Bale told Mira about the train as Mira worked on dinner. Before they sat to eat, they tied Mira's mother to a chair.

"Does it hurt her?" Bale asked.

"The tying?"

"The moon being gone. Like it does to Murk?"

"Nah. She gets kind of lively really. We don't tie her down, she'll get up and try dancing but fall over."

They went to the kitchen and Mira served Bale rabbit soup. "Like it?"

Food was a miracle to Bale. Something as ordinary as salty broth. Gigantically thin. Impossibly simple. "Rabbits don't look like they'd taste this good."

Mira ate roasted carrots and celery. Golden-brown blisters, shimmering iridescent. She picked at her food with a fork.

"There not enough for both of us?"

"There was," said Mira. "More if you want. I just can't eat rabbit. Mom can, but it's not for me."

Bale slowed his eating. "Well, you cook it good."

"Thanks."

From the other room, they could hear Mira's mother groan.

"Where does Murk go?"

"Who knows? If you wander around in the nights like these, you hear people screaming pain near everywhere. Distantly, most times, but the draining makes most folks flop off wherever. Mom used to call it fright night."

Bale pulled a bone from the stew, was about to gnaw on it. "What about what I said earlier? About Jessup and his dad."

"It'd be nice if we could fix her. It's why I went to the train the last time. She wanted me to see about a cure."

"And the first time? With the flowers."

"Citrus blossoms."

"Citrus blossoms," Bale repeated her. "Any of them ever quit shadows? Like, in the morning, when Murk wakes up, he'll be normal?"

"As normal as he gets, maybe. He'll look like dog shit and feel like it too, and then he'll find his shadow and be right back where he was."

"What if it's cloudy?"

"The sun'll come out eventually."

"So, once a month they shut down. Become defenseless basically. Why did people have to go into the domes at all? Why didn't they just wait for a new moon and catch 'em while they drained?"

"Mom says they did. Years ago. They wrangled people up while they drained. Mom says it's why the domes exist. Like they were made for shadow addicts. The trains too."

"Serious?"

"That's what she says. But people heard they were killing each other. Killing themselves. Inside. And people outside just drank more shadows."

"I've never heard that, but I guess it's possible."

"She might be wrong too, but she says they flip-flopped it. Addicts and their families stayed out. All the good people went in."

They ate. The muddled sound of chewing. Fork tines and spoon tips against porcelain, tink-tinkling.

After a moment, Mira said, "Even if it's true about the shadows and comets, about what you heard from that man. I don't know Mom's thief, who to even start looking for. And, if I found them, I don't really see myself as a killer."

"Murk and I could do it." Bale's matter-of-fact eyes.

"You don't know where you're at, and Murk is somewhere screaming cusses at the night."

"It's worth a try. If we find who did it, and it works. And she gets better. No more shade trading."

Mira scooted her vegetables. Her fork clink-clinking. "We can ask if she remembers, but I'm not sure she does."

AFTER DINNER, THEY stood on the porch, stared up at the night. "It's crazy y'all have 'em."

"What?"

"The stars."

Back in the dome, they'd taught about night. They said there were people who could tell your future based on the stars that were out when you were born. Bale didn't know what stars he was born beneath, but he hoped they were the good-future kind. He thought: tonight, they shine for me. And the comet coming made them shine even brighter.

The Draining

Dark, dark night. In a bitter state, Murk thrashed, his body scrunched back into chest-high foliage, wriggling against the earth and mashing grass blades beneath him. He wretched and he wrestled, grabbed handfuls of anything his hands landed on.

The black veins beneath his skin began to bleed their color through his flesh, which darkened back from pale, and as the blackness slipped out his pores, it whispered away as vapor might. The scent of it like urine, and Murk trembled in the stench, his tongue foul-stuck to the backs of his teeth, his jaw aching as though locked tight.

He sat prone. Rocking. "Shitty fucking shit," Murk said. "Shitty, shit, shitty."

three

For every black magic that infects the world, a miracle occurs to offset it. There came another way to make a shadow gone. A young girl discovered the trick, though she couldn't fully articulate it. She could simply make the thing disappear with her mind. It was a condition, like balance. A sense, like smell. But she could guide others into the performance.

Word spread and followers flocked. They formed some shadowless army.

Ranks of women gathered in formation, their shadows hidden from the gaze of the world, their long hair braided behind them, moving in near silence. They shouldered rifles, rubbed ash around their eyes.

Most of these soldiers once had mothers who'd been molested, thieved from, who'd lost their shadows, their ability to sleep. They'd been raised on lies, told, "Inside the dome, they're working to fix it." But the fix never materialized.

And then the trains came.

Into the wilderness, a slow-motion invasion, moving over chewed-up tracks, a recycled procession.

The female army sought vengeance for false myths. They swept through the world like organized catastrophe, a plague on the train-circled dwellings. They machined over the outposts, blundering the trains, murdering the domers. They hoarded rifles and swords, gunpowder and coal. They built catapults that heaved rudimentary explosives. They invaded in broad daylight or whistled through in the darkness. They shrieked and hollered, howled and yelped. Spat curses, bit cheeks, ran knives across throats.

Hardened animals—stern women with certain eyes. Nomads who slept in tent cities like warring Visigoths, chanting violent hymns to deities they invented in their images. The flavor of their murderous lust an electricity that bound them to their missions. And they took no prisoners, save for one.

The Morning After

The sun was up, so the dark could start. Everywhere, men and women dragged themselves into the light from wallows and hovels, from snag crooks and mishap holes to drop, once again, into the stupor the sun gave them. Murk was among these. He woke in grass, his wooden leg clutched to his chest, his hair messed and crazed. His eyelids smiled open and then his mouth. He blinked fiercely. He gulped at air. Using the fake leg like a cane, he hopped to his foot, and hopping thusly, sprang into the day and found a nice flat bit of dirt to guzzle his shadow from. "A world with two suns," he sang, "that is the dream." He beamed at the sun, "You sweet bitch," he told it. He gaped at his shade. "I always tell you," he told it, "I always say just stay inside me." The shadow stared back, silent. "But you always leave." Murk pointed down at the thing as though it were alive. "I know it's not your fault," he told it, "but still." He dropped to the earth, sort of stroked his shadow with the back of a finger. "Should we get to it?" he asked. He didn't wait for a response. "A world with two suns," he sang. Then he placed his mouth to the dimness, his lips on the dirt. He slurped it the way those from the coast slurped oysters from their shells, ingurgitating the darkness, sloshing up dirt in his spittle that crunched between his teeth. Immediately, his skin paled. His eyes began their darkening. "That is the dream," he sang when the drinking was done.

He stood on one leg. His veins dark through his pale flesh. He wanted to fly.

"The train," he said. And, with his leg still not yet attached, he attempted to run, fell face down on the ground, began hysterically laughing. He crawled on the ground to his peg, rolled to his back and strapped it on snug.

Once it was on, he did his best to spring erect. Disoriented a bit, he spun slowly trying to place himself. He held up a finger. "The train?" He glared. He pointed. "That way." And he took off—the sort of singsong jog of a false-legged man.

The Shadowless
Chaperones

The Founder of the Shadowless Army had a son with a domer. It was scandalous. She took the father hostage after they sacked a train because he had pretty red hair and she kept him as a concubine. He told her that the domers were sterilized before leaving, so when she got pregnant, she killed him.

The Founder did her best to keep the child hid. He didn't leave her tent for years, toddling to and fro under the supervision of lesser soldiers. She never even hugged him.

Raised like that, the boy grew irksome. Once able, he would decamp and run ungoverned through the world, vandalizing whatever he could.

The older women soldiers called him Huck Finn—all old books were curses to them. When he showed up black eyed and shadowless, no one was surprised. They drugged the boy and hacked off his leg. Legless addicts seemed to behave better, but he remained a little asshole.

Three soldiers were enlisted as his chaperones. They were flunkies in the ranks. Mole, the most senior member, had been caught crying on the battlefield. Jilly was such a profane and reckless soldier her superiors half thought her a man in disguise. Baby Boo was new to service, and, like all recruits, had taken a yearlong vow of silence to show her loyalty to the cause.

They all hated their job.

"Man, I tell you what," Jilly said, "I'd cut the little fucker's head off and bury it in sand. Blow torch that sand into glass, take the rest of his body drizzle it with honey and set that on an ant hill, poison them fucking ants once they ate him up." She looked like she'd eat a lightbulb on a dare. She had only recently completed her year of silence and seemed always to be making up for lost conversation.

"You talk too much," said Mole. She had patient, hospitable eyes. She had heart in her voice. But she had also stomped a brain out a skull before. Glared down at the gray matter twinkling in the sunshine, proudly.

"Shit, I ain't said a fucking thing in a year or nothing. Kept my tongue stuck to my teeth and didn't even whisper shit into my pillow like Baby Boo do. Forgive me if my mouth gets to going free, but I assume you was the same way when they told you you could talk again."

"You talk this much before?"

"If I had something worth saying I'd say it and no one could tell me not to unless they wanted more than just words with me, and then I'd oblige them on that front too, cause I ain't never been afraid of nothing except sharks and roaches, and I don't get in the ocean and I shake my shirts and shoes before I wear 'em."

They trailed the redhead's wayward destruction, dragging him back to the Founder every so often just to prove that the boy was alive, and it was a thankless gig they had.

They followed him in a patient way. The faster they caught him, the sooner they'd lose him again. They'd corral him on home to see his mother, and she'd look at him absently and the cycle began anew.

He was lost, and they were after him.

"We had a crazed steer that my mom cut the balls off. Maybe that would help this fucker to calm. When we catch him again let's try it." Jilly was chomping chewing gum that she'd pilfered from some ruined town they'd passed through. She blew bubbles on occasion. Smacked and popped like as if for attention.

"You had a crazed bull," said Mole. The two walked side by side, didn't make eye contact when they spoke. Up ahead, Baby Boo moved in silence.

"Don't tell me what the fuck I had. I was there, I saw it."

"It's logistics," Mole said. "Bulls got balls, steers do not. Y'all made him a steer."

Jilly popped a bubble. "Well, let's make this little fucker a steer then."

"I don't know we can."

"Sure we can. We'll tell his mom he caught his nuts on whatever, that it wasn't us did it per se. 'We found him that way, ma'am,' I'll tell her. Keep the things in a jar just in case he wants to hold 'em as mementos."

"It's not that. And we're not supposed to say she's his mom." Mole took a tube of salve from her pocket, dabbed a bit on her palm, rubbed her face with it, offered some to Jilly.

Jilly scowled at the stuff. "Fuck no." She blew a bubble.

"What I mean is, you cut the nuts off a bull, it's a steer. Cut the nuts off a boy, I don't know what it becomes."

"It becomes better than it was."

They came to a long-dilapidated paint store, its front windows recently broken open. There were tracks in the dirt. One shoe print, one peg poke. Jilly dropped down on her knees to eye them. "A few days back I reckon."

The odor of the place was noxious. "We're looking for paint," Mole said. "Let's go before the fumes melt our brains."

Outside, Jilly held out her hand. "I changed my mind. Give me some of that shit you rub on your face."

"Not unless you ask nice."

"Fuck it then."

They walked on, came to a building less than a half block away and on it was a crudely painted skull with hashtags for eyes.

Jilly spat at it. "Only something with nuts would've ever painted that."

Haircut

Bale woke on the couch again, but this time the house stood still. He was back in his teensy shorts, his itty-bitty V-neck. He cleared his throat, rubbed his eyes, stretched his hands—the crisscross of veins and tendons, the knuckles. He made fists, jabbed the air. Rolled his head, cracked his neck. Got up, his shirt riding up over his belly button. He walked to the stereo as Murk had done the day before but had never worked one and didn't want to upset it. He peeked in the kitchen—empty. He headed to the bathroom and took a piss. The plumbing worked on well water, you could tell by the smell of it. The same sort of mineral stench of the water they had behind the train. The bowl of the toilet thick with deposits where the water line rose to. There must have been a windmill pump around and Bale credited Mira's deceased father with its install. Maybe they were plumber's clothes that he wore the previous day. Behind the train they had a few turbines. They had cisterns for the crops, but it so rarely rained that they needed the wells. Bale wondered how the crops were doing. He didn't know much about what they'd planted, but every so often he'd turn his binoculars on the rows, try to calculate the plants' growth.

"Mira," he called out after washing his hands, stepping out the bathroom. "Mira."

Nothing. He went to the front door. His hand on the knob of the thing, he thought about what Murk said. The Doors? Had he heard them? The album cover. The haircut.

Bale scrubbed at his hair. For the first time in his whole life, he could decide how to cut it. In the dome administrators decided all that, and the administrators were never unseated. If they died, their offspring supplanted them. They figured the less choices you made the better. But now, Bale could choose.

He opened the door, and Mira stood in the sun in her short robe tending her mother. She set a finger to her lips—Bale liked when she shushed him—whispered when she got near. "Woke up early to get her a shadow so she'd sleep. You okay?" Mira stepped back into the house and Bale followed, ogling where her shadow should be.

"I'm fantastic," he said.

"I was gonna make agua de jamaica, ever had it?"

"Huh-what?"

"It's hibiscus flowers. Like tea. But I've never had tea. Just read about it in books. You ever had tea?"

"No. But I've had coffee and I think that's sort of like tea."

"Maybe. You'll like this. It's pink."

"Great," said Bale. "It'll match how my shorts make me feel." He held his hands out like a performer, tried to grin all his charm. "I got a question."

"Okay." They went to the kitchen and Mira did her banging

around thing—began to heat water, dragged down a container of dried flowers.

"Will you cut my hair?"

"You don't like it?"

"I don't think so. Do you?"

Mira took two white mugs from the cabinet and set them on the counter. They didn't quite match, but it was close. "I've never seen you any other way."

"Me either," said Bale. "That's the point."

Mira went to him. "What would you want?"

"I think something kind of different. Know what a Mohawk is? You cut off all this." He covered the sides of his head with his hands. "Just leave the strip on the top."

"I know what a Mohawk is."

"Can you do one?"

She passed her fingers through his hair, and the kettle hissed steam. She plucked the thing from the stove, poured hot water in the mugs. "I think. But first let's drink this."

Drummond Unwinding

Through the pierced roof, Drummond watched a redheaded boy climb through the refuse. He carried a paint can and brush and he marked skulls on any flat surface he saw. There seemed a comedy in his movements. Drummond decided to appeal to him.

"You there," Drummond called, and his voice shocked the painter, and the painter came to him.

"What's that?" He looked like the kind of boy who'd kick a kitten.

"I'm trapped. Could you lend a hand?"

The painter scratched his head, touched the sheet metal before him, pulled the brush from his bucket and began to paint. "What's in it for me?"

Drummond thought. "Well, I'm naked. I got nothing. So . . . gratefulness."

"You got something."

Drummond checked his naked body. "What's that?"

"A shadow. I'll let you out of there if you give it to me."

"Give it to you?"

"Let me drink it off the ground." The painter stepped back from the hole through which he and Drummond spoke, found his shadow. "Watch," he said. Then he set his paint bucket on the dirt, lowered himself and drank. When he raised up, his eyes were black. He winked one of them at Drummond and made his head balloon twice its size, his eyes spread out like saucers. He laughed a thin laughter, resumed normal form.

Drummond said, "Fuck."

The painter took his bucket back in hand. "If you don't like the conditions, you're free to free yourself." He determined the sun's line. "You'll get a shadow in there eventually. Swallow it, slip through that hole." He marked more with his brush.

Drummond sat on his bare ass, "Thanks anyhow," he said, his voice echoing out into the air.

"No problem."

More Disaster

He could smell it before anything. He could taste the ash in the air. The gunpowder. The murder. Tears came to his eyes. In his earliest darkened state, he was much like a child. If a whim presented itself, and then was not fulfilled, his emotions tattered and blew piecemeal like shrapnel. Nostalgia stirred deep in his soul, a piteous ache. This train was his thing.

As he approached, he whispered invocations, pleading with whatever existent deity there might be that his senses deceived him.

He stumbled forward. His teeth clattered in his mouth. His blackened-out eyes nervous in their sockets.

When he got there, it looked like a snake pulled from its coil and thrashed against a boulder until dead, left to fall where it would. A kind of horror struck him.

Murk slowpoked his way on. He felt filthy and grief-stricken. Doleful and smote. He half wished he believed in some true God to appeal to. Once his mother had told him of God, but on her deathbed she'd laughed off the idea.

"Sure," she gleamed. "Up there," she pointed. "A man who looks out for all this." She wanded her hand toward the catastrophe of existence. And ever since then Murk was sure humanity stood indefensible.

Murk walked toward the train, the shadow poison inside him.

Breezed ash drifted across the scape. Motes of char curled into braids. Murk dragged onward into the oppressive imagery, the frightening reality of it. Train cars were heaped catawampus, willy-nilly. Cockeyed corpses clung to knotted wads of rubbish. Dross seemed the standard. An obscure crackling preached out from the myriad fires dwindling. The stained smell of death lingered. The hollow feel of defeat or doom.

Murk turned aft, and, in the distance, he saw a little person perched near one of the toppled train cars marking the side of the thing with a crudely painted skull. Hashtags for eyes. His hair red. And Murk called out to him, "You." At that, the redhead dropped his paintbrush and gave flight. His movements recognizable to Murk. The redhead had a false leg.

Murk gave chase. The two amputees hobbling in oddball fashion—one fleeing, one in pursuit. And, as they moved, Murk continued to call. "Stop. Stop. I only got questions." This, however, was a lie. Murk had a rage that needed placing. He had questions as well, but he figured he could twine the things together.

Murk, larger than his prey, of longer stride, immediately gained. "I'm gonna catch you eventually."

"Tongue my ass," cried the redhead.

"Just as soon as you quit moving."

They dragged away from the dilapidated train, into a prairie pocked with cactus and Mexican palmettos. It was a hokey-dokey kind of chase that resulted in Murk grabbing a tuft of the painter's red hair from behind, dragging him to the earth and holding him to it.

"You're just a boy," said Murk, and the child spat at him. Murk punched him twice in the face, and black blood erupted from his nose, his dark eyes winced.

He ballooned himself then, and the expansion of his body forced Murk from his frame, and the boy rose, his skin sprawled into that configuration only shadow addicts could achieve, and he tarried forward with the wind, the breezes pushing him along like a sail, but Murk stood and puffed up as well, his distended form also propelled by gusts, and the bloated monopods slipped across the landscape like discarded tissues, huffing along in rapid heaves.

Again Murk's size afforded him an advantage. Through the grainy world they flew, but Murk overtook the boy, wrapped him in his clutches, dragged him to the grass and yanked off his false leg. The boy laid back, deflated, and Murk stood above him holding the wood leg like a club.

"What do you want?"

"Heard about you," said Murk, and he slipped back to true form. "You're a thief."

The boy laughed fake laughter.

"What happened to the train?"

"Got what was coming to it?" The boy dabbed then at his bloody nose.

"You did all that?"

"Look at me. That was an army. A great army led by a great leader that did that."

Murk eyed him. He was a fragile thing, but he was proud. "You know Jessup?"

The boy shrugged. "Might."

"He's got a theory 'bout you."

"Who gives a shit?"

"A friend of mine," Murk said. Then he brought the leg down on the boy's skull and the boy's face went oblong. Murk swung again and the boy's eye socket sunk, vomited out the eyeball, the thing belching open. Murk swung again and the whole thing chopped through, opened up. Revealed a blackened brain that slunk out from the breakage. Murk brought the leg down again and it slurped into the stew of his used-to-be head.

He raised it, the peg leg. Looked at the black bloodstain, which slowly grew in color, made its way back to crimson. It seemed to glow beneath the pale blue sky above. Murk mulled over the dead thing at his feet. It reminded him so much of himself, he couldn't help but hate it.

Bale the Shade Trader

Earlier that morning, before Bale's haircut, Mira had asked her mother who'd done it. "Your shadow?" Mira said, "the man? Who was he?"

"I had it once," her mother said. She pointed to the ground. "It was right here."

"I know where it would be if you had it, and I was with you before it was gone and there when it was taken."

"You were?"

Mira's eyes seemed to slice her mother's throat. "Maybe you need more sleep."

"Weren't you bringing me something? From a gull?"

"I tried yesterday. Couldn't find one."

"Endless water," her mother said. "It's a beautiful rest. Refreshing."

"She's jobbing you," said Bale.

"If I bring you a gull shadow," Mira asked, "will you remember?"

Mira's mother frowned. "Couldn't hurt," she said.

• • •

Bale and Mira went out looking. Somehow, his Mohawk made Bale's clothes seem more his own—they intentionally fit snug.

Mira and Bale chattered as they hunted.

"We had cats in the dome," Bale said. "I always wondered what they were thinking."

"They're assholes," Mira told him. "They think riddles."

"But you can talk to them."

"I guess. I mean, I don't ever take away much from it."

"We kept them so they'd eat rats. Ever talked to a rat?"

They had made way into a field thick with cactus that they had to weave carefully through. "No," said Mira.

"Snake?"

"No."

"What's the animal best to talk with?"

"Usually people," Mira said.

"Usually?"

"Sometimes they ask too many questions."

At noon, they stopped to eat cornbread with goat-milk butter. They sat in the shade of a grapefruit tree, the fruit too green to pick. "These are good when they're ripe," said Mira. "And they'll be ripe soon. Used to, this whole area was used for farming them. There'd be rows and rows, for miles, my dad said. They're bitter and sweet and sting your lips, but in a good way."

Inch-long thorns protruded from the limbs. "Looks mean. Smells nice though."

"Thorns are to keep away the rats."

"Which you've never talked to."

Mira chewed on bread. "I have. I've swallowed rat shadow. I've talked to them. Not a source of pride, I don't guess."

"Is that one?" Bale asked. In the sky, a gray bird circled passively.

Mira dropped her cornbread in the dirt, pounced to her feet and was running. "C'mon," she hollered, and Bale followed her, the two sprinting toward the bird.

The thing kited up and down, cawed a comic tone and Mira and Bale did their best to put it between them and the sun, having to alternate their gazes from the sky where it was to the ground where its likeness would be, all the while dancing about clumsily in attempts to dodge parched, green cactus paddles thorned with bright yellow needles. It was not a swift bird, but it seemed aware of Bale and Mira's intentions and bounced around on the breezes evading their attempts at pilfering.

"Tell it to stop."

"So we can make it like my mother?"

Just then, Bale tripped on a crag, plunged to the dirt. He rolled to his back. "Lie to it."

"Wait," said Mira. She ran back to the grapefruit tree, and, when she returned, Bale was up on his feet chasing the bird. "Watch," she told him. She tossed a hunk of cornbread at the bird, and it dipped in the sky, caught the bread in flight. The next bit she threw drew the gull closer. It had vacant, hungry eyes. It chipped wildly. Wherever Mira tossed bread, the bird went. She seemed to have it trained that way, and, as Mira fed the thing, Bale moved stealth-like to find the bird's shadow pitching across the dirt.

"I just suck it up?"

Mira tossed another bit of bread. "Yeah, but don't swallow it. Hold it in your cheeks."

"Does it taste like anything?"

"Nothing you'd know the taste of."

When Bale sipped from the earth, the bird hooted a hurt tone, and Mira tossed bread, but the gull let it fall. It spread its wings, clung to some new draft and pulled away from them. Bale watched it fly toward the direction of the gulf, his cheeks bloated with the thing's nasty-flavored shade.

WHEN THEY GOT back, Bale was surprised there was any shade left in his mouth at all—he could feel himself accidentally swallowing it as they advanced.

"Did you get it?" Mira's mother asked. "Were you able?"

"Yes, Momma," said Mira, "we did," but this surprised her mother.

"You're talking," she said. "How you got it and talking?"

"Bale's got it. Don't worry. Bale," said Mira, as if hurrying him to spit the thing in her mother's mouth.

But Bale hesitated. He felt silly. Mohawk and bulging cheeks. He looked down at Mira' mother, noticed her scarecrow-dancing eyes, her skin, pale and grimy. He kind of shook his head no.

"What's wrong?" But Mira quickly understood.

She leaned to him. It wasn't a kiss, but Bale felt her lips on his lips, softly parted, could smell the warmth of her. With her gentle mouth on his mouth, Bale breathed into her slow, and Mira's eyes smiled at him, and she bent to her mother. And poof: her mother was asleep.

Drummond's Escape

The evening sun bled in through the cargo-car ceiling and Drummond watched his likeness on the floor. It was so easy. He could walk straight up to it. His belly ached, his tongue stuck to his teeth. For all he knew, his brother was dead. He was fairly certain all others in the camp were. How else would they have just let the redheaded fucker move through painting on shit? He had to do something or he would die. The car smelled of Drummond's shit, which sat in a lowly heap in the corner, and, behind that odor, the tangy vinegar of stagnant piss which pooled and ran in streams. The flavor thickened Drummond's throat, and he wondered if the shadow would wash it down, he wondered if it could set him free.

Drummond's bare feet, dirty with his own filth.

The last time he pissed, he'd half thought of cupping his hand in the stream for a swallow of it. He shrugged, "Better than dying to death." He placed his lips against the wall and drank his shadow.

He felt it first in his skull, as though he were sucking a thick liquid through a straw and the pressure of it squeezed his head. A warmth spread deep in him. His shoulders seemed to flutter with light. Then his back. He stepped away, lowered his head toward his navel. For a moment, he thought he'd be pulled into the fetal position, thought he'd drop from his feet and grovel on the ground, but no. A quick contraction pulled him tight and let go, as though he were merely a hand quickly trying to clap alone.

A joyous sensation. It sillied the mind. Lassoing those odd patterns into phrases would be impossible.

Let us say that he felt like a great ship pushed from a dock and into the ocean for the first time, so that he'd seemed to have always rested on the wrong surface and had now found his true home. Sure he'd been built elsewhere, but he'd been made for this.

His eyes went stark and his skin paled and his veins darkened, as were the symptoms, and Drummond gazed back at the sun, which he could see through the torn-open roof, and it seemed truer than he'd ever known it, and a mellow sort of prayer chanced his mind, and then Drummond, as if by force beyond him, was drawn to the opening, and he smoothly squeezed through it.

He was then in the open. In the deeper light. In the smell of fire.

He ballooned. He felt the wind on him. He began running.

He felt like a child.

He kited forward.

He was alive.

Murk the Murderer

Murk came to the door, stood with the bloodied peg leg in his hand.

Bale pointed, "What's that?"

Murk raised the peg leg. "A murder weapon."

"Who you after?" Mira asked.

"Already aftered him. He was painting those skulls."

"The fella Jessup was after?"

"I think so."

"Then Jessup owes us even more. Where'd you find him?"

"That's the thing," said Murk. "He was painting on your train."

Bale thought on this. "My train?"

"It's fucked," said Murk. "Like the one from yesterday, just fresher. Fires still smoldering."

Bale grabbed his rifle. Bale ran out the door.

Black-eyed Children

Mole, Jilly, and Baby Boo chased the graffiti across the coun-tryside, finding it on water towers and felled train cars, painted skulls on tree trunks and the doors of abandoned houses.

"It's never taken this long," Mole said.

"Shit. We becoming worse soldiers?" asked Jilly.

They saw a small posse of shadow sippers in a prairie and Jilly scoped them in her rifle.

They were boys at play. Four of them rascaling about. They had a ball they were wrestling over.

One boy would get hold of it and run, the others trying to strip it away. If it came loose another would take up a turn. Their laughter floated like any laughter would. It wasn't stained black like their eyes.

"I'm gonna shoot one," said Jilly.

Mole gaped at her. "Why?"

"To prove I still can. I ain't seen combat in forever."

"It's a bad idea."

Baby Boo listened to see what the verdict might be. Her moony eyes gleaming.

"It's not like they're gonna grow up and grow out of it," said Jilly. "They'll get worse and hurt others with their worsening."

The Shadowless Army didn't attack shadow addicts as a primary function, but when they got in the way, they'd knock them over.

"We don't have orders to, and they're not bothering us."

"Shit, Mole. I'm bored. Out here. All this damn nothing but walking."

Mole looked at Jilly and Baby Boo. They seemed to encourage her with their eyes. To whisper, *let us at them*, with their thoughts. Mole watched the boys at play. In the grand scheme of things, what were they even worth?

"Don't use any bullets," she said, and Mole barely had the words out of her mouth when Jilly led the charge. Baby Boo followed closely. Mole trailed them.

Bored soldiers slaughtering the innocent predates the naming of war, will go on after the words we call it are broken. But the glistening of their bayonets, the lads with their hands fumbling at their spilled entrails, the shrieking and their grievous, black eyes. Some echo of that injustice will travel out with the expanding universe, get back to God if there is one, become a thing we're remembered for forever.

Mole thought about that as she watched her warriors whetting their appetites for pain. She pouted toward heaven. Shrugged to say, "If you didn't want it, it wouldn't be." Then she raised the butt of her rifle and brought it down against the skull of one of them. Who was she to judge?

Baby Boo kicked their bloodied ball and the thing bounced across the field, and Jilly laughed as it went bouncing.

Drummond's Death

Bale walked the debris, kicking this and that, tapping his rifle barrel against charred cadavers, against refuse caked with ash that broke to reveal sun-colored embers. Gray blankets of smoke drifted casually from sinking fires. The stillness of it got to him, his jaw ached and his chest shimmied and he swallowed stiffly.

"You didn't see anyone alive?"

Murk stood off at some distance, panting. "You knew I followed you?"

"Could hear you from the start, that wood peg tap-tapping."

"Only saw the redhead." Murk pointed with the bloodied wooden leg. "He's over there."

Bale glanced back at Murk, off in the pointed direction. "You check him?"

"Check him?"

"His pockets and stuff?"

Murk held the bloodstained false appendage. "I got his leg."

"Show me the rest of him."

The two walked to where the murder had occurred, both

silent as though partway sleeping. The gray-going world seemed to suffer from nausea. No wind stirred, but smoke drifted. The smell of it pleasant, somehow.

"Made work of him," Bale said, looking down at the boy's broke-open head.

Murk lobbed the peg leg toward the battered brains. "I was agitated."

Bale reached down to check his pockets, but kind of staggered. "I'm woozy," he said and he leaned on his rifle like a cane. He pointed at the boy. "Look him." He couldn't quite form sentences.

Murk fidgeted his fingers into the crevices of the dead boy's clothes, coming up with a few trinkets that seemed like make-shift playthings. Some twine. A small glass bottle. A petrified frog. "What am I looking for?"

"Something that seems like it should be found."

Murk stood when the job was done, contemplated the pile of plucked-up things. "None of this meets that description." Bale frowned. Murk felt his disappointment, pain. "If you want," he said, "we can go back through, look for whoever. I'll help you bury folks."

Bale straightened up. Held his rifle like a soldier should. "Bury?"

"Sure," said Murk, "putting the dead in the ground. You domers don't do it?"

"Nah. Never heard of it. What's the point?"

Murk swept his tongue across the front of his gray teeth. "Fuck if I know. Something to do, I guess."

"I don't care much for digging," Bale said. "Back home we burn the bodies." The fires fumed. "Someone's already done that bit for us. I had a brother in that mess somewhere. Didn't figure I'd see him again ever. I guess now I know for sure."

"Should we say something over it?"

Bale stared at Murk. "I just did."

"But, like, to your God or something?"

"Thanks a lot, God," said Bale. Then, "Did you want to add something?"

Murk shifted. "I like your haircut."

"Not what I meant, but thanks." The sky darkened. "Don't you dare fucking steal it."

Most times, Murk would've argued. Instead, they walked back to Mira's house in silence.

Drummond Thirsts

Drummond needed food, water. His head spun in the new daze of his foreign state. His vision puttered and shimmied and his ears seemed reshaped so that every sound registered as something exotic, remote. His own feet against the earth, for instance, reverberated, buzzed, signaled out echoes that seemed to race in every direction and this cacophony spooked Drummond into believing he was continuously followed. Smells had been similarly reinvented to him. His odor, ripe and fetid, perched him in a kind of smog of stench. The milky perfume of his reek seemed thick enough to chew on, blow bubbles with. Every time he swallowed, the flavor, as thick as grease, seemed to scrape down his throat, slump in his guts. The night sat heavy on him. Humid dark stretched infinitely above and he felt a column of it weighting his shoulders, crowning his head. Walking meant parting the chunky, black air, creating a wake that rippled out behind as he moved. Each star was a needle of light aimed at his eyes, but all things were one.

He sensed the trees breathing, grass alive. He knew where

birds would fly from. Their courses were patterned out before them like dotted lines. Like bits of bread they followed the trail of.

Drummond could see his own path too. He was pulled forward as if by his nose, and he could nearly see the force pulling him. Shapeless but present. Steady but ungoverned.

For hours he moved, over grasses he swore could talk to him, between clusters of trees he was certain were fucking. Birds chirped at him and it was as if their music swam down his ears, danced in his brain.

Some time passed before he realized he knew where he was going. Somehow, his nose had found water. His body ballooned, his skin scant, stretched. "I'm a beast," he said to himself, but his voice bled from him shrill, seemed to cast blue fire, skipped off like fairy flight. He giggled at it, and gray rings of laughter spread out and dissipated.

He maneuvered on in his newfound way. His thoughts were shallow puddles of this and that. Nothing lasted longer than a breath. Knickknack nouns rummaged by bric-a-brac verbs.

"Hello!" he shouted at himself. The letters of the word floated into the stars, became a constellation. Twinkled.

He climbed a hill. The moon grinned from high. His naked body gleamed in the grin of it.

At the top of the hill, he surveyed the crater. At the bottom of the hill, a pond showed the moon again. Two smiles—one above, one below. He stepped toward the lower one, lost his footing, went skidding in the dirt, racing as he rolled, head over heels, clumping toward the bottom, toward the water.

The ground leveled before he reached the crater pond's edge.

He came to a stall on his back, eyed his ribs, rubbed raw by the earth. Rashes seemed to spring on his flesh. He touched them, sticky against his fingers. A dull ache traced his wholeness. Each breath stung, but was flavored by the brackish water nearby. He rolled to his belly, dug his elbows in the mud. Edging forward as a snake might, slipping into the ooze of moist earth and scum, he pulled his body to the water's edge, placed his lips against the cool, dark surface, slurped earth and liquid into his mouth, chewed the swallows across his dried lips, leathery tongue.

He felt crazy in his drinking, the water had ahold of him. It seemed he'd drink until he drowned, as though he'd never be able to pause for breath.

Lust forced him forward, and he moved on into the pond, until he felt weightless, bobbed on the surface like a loose blade of grass.

He rolled to his back, ran his fingers through his sweat-thickened hair, let his head sink. He kicked out deeper. The splashes of his swimming sang out into the crater, mirrored out into the night. A vast, indigo universe straggled above toward forever, and Drummond's gaze wandered amongst the stars. Not all of them were white, but Drummond couldn't think the names of the colors. A rage paddled across his heart. His jaw tensed. There, floating limp in the crater puddle, he squinted at the sky. He reached his fingers at the stars he couldn't remember the colors of, made as if to snuff them away.

The Name

Mira stood in the doorway, watched Murk and Bale drag their feet. She held a pitcher of water, chill, slightly cloudy, pulled up from the well. It had a mineral flavor, a prolonged aftertaste of earth. She filled a glass, held it out for the first to get to her, and Bale jogged forward toward it, grabbed it and guzzled. As he drank, Mira poured a glass for Murk. He took it, sipped at it, swished and swallowed. Sipped some more.

"Was the train . . ." Mira began, but Bale avoided her eyes.

He lowered his glass toward her to be refilled, breathed heavily, "Your mom remember the name?"

Mira took the glass, decided Bale wasn't being himself, poured him more water. "She thinks she does." The sound of the water stopped. Bale took the glass back, drank again. "But I don't know where he'd be. But that's not all. I looked in my mom's almanac, and it shows that comet's coming. So the folks you met couldn't be all wrong."

"But who is it?" Murk asked, his upper lip wet with well water. "The thief?"

"Joe Clover," Mira said.

Murk snickered. "Figures," he said.

"Why's that?" said Bale.

"Cause all Joe Clover wants is shadows and shadows and shadows again. If he were a dog, he wouldn't come to your knees. But he's all teeth and claws. He says he was six when he drank shadow the first time. His own mother's. Since then, he's just been tussling around with bad intentions. Hangs out a place called the Lost Souls."

"Let's go to town then," said Bale.

Mira and Murk seemed traumatized by Bale's suggestion.

Drummond Again

From a distance, he probably seemed dead. Nude. Afloat. His eyes wildly staring off. Something so lost about them now. Black, sure, but the domestic tone they used to have, lost worse than dead languages are lost.

But it's the music of language, mutely finding his submerged ears, that forces him to reconfigure, roll to his belly, tread water meekly so his nose and eyes peer from the pond. Some man-shaped amphibian that indigenous people would dream up to scare their children with.

Along the shore, there were figures. Drummond spotted some cattails and breaststroked toward them. He moved as near silent as he could. Tucked himself amongst the weeds and hid there.

From that vantage, he considered those across the body from him. They lowered their faces to the water and drank. Their drinking made Drummond jealous. It was his water. He thought. All of it.

Across the water, near the shore, several huts of grass and tree limbs stood caked with mud that must have come from the pond bottom. In and out of these huts, people hobbled. Drummond watched them build a pit fire. Watched them cooking beasts in the flames, smoke belching up toward the sun. If he was hungry for the flesh of the things, he didn't sense it, but he did gulp water, wallow in the weeds, piss when the need took him.

There he stayed sprawled and offended at his own mind's ineptitude. He marveled at nothing, and the day did its doing. The sun wilted toward evening.

The syrupy conditions that took hold were made wicked by his confusion. He hated his own shadow for being in him and promised himself he'd never drink the thing again.

Drummond watched the sun as it set. Watched it so hard it seemed to dance toward him, a circle of fire, swimming in rhythms at its edges.

He whispered, "Fuck you," at it.

It slowly slipped off.

Time passed.

The sky went dark again.

The Searching Platoon

For Mole, Jilly, and Baby Boo the redhead's trail dried up.

"Let's just end this business," said Jilly. She was rubbing Mole's salve on her cheeks. "We go back and say, 'Ma'am, your son got himself dead somehow and we weren't there to see it. Terribly sorry for your loss,' and if she takes it too hard we can blame it on Baby Boo."

"I imagine she'd know it's a lie," said Mole. "And let's not call him that."

"Call him what? Her son? What else you call him? I'm not calling him Huck Finn. I heard that book read to me once and I liked that character more than to bless his name on some runt like that boy, and she's not a deity as far as I can tell, or she'd have had better offspring, and you can tell her I said it if you want, and if I'm wrong she can strike me down with lightning bolts or whatever awesome power she possesses."

"We don't know he's hers for sure. It's speculation, sort of. I mean, she doesn't call him her son. Not that anyone's heard anyhow."

"Well what the hell else would he be? Her cousin? I had a cousin when I was young and I pushed him off a rooftop just to hear the sound of him against the ground, and I've met her and she's meaner than me. Shit, she makes me look like I got angel wings on my pussy."

"I don't want Baby Boo to hear you talking like that."

Jilly ordered Baby Boo to go get a campfire lit. Jilly sort of whispered to Mole, "Ain't like I'm inciting here. Founder tells me to die for the cause, I'll take a flaming arrow through each titty, but this ain't the cause. This is babysitting. And I coulda stayed babysitting where I was. It've been safe. Just hauling shadow spits for my momma and helping to make sure my brothers didn't fuck the family goats." She tossed Mole's salve to her.

"Fine," said Mole. "It's not the best, but our time will come."

"Our time for what? In a few minutes Baby Boo will come back with a low-hung head cause she's too stupid to light a fire and I'll have to go fix the situation by rubbing goddamned sticks together, and I'm not supposed to have to rub sticks no more and then we'll lie around by the fire at night, just you and me telling each other the same bullshit stories."

"You don't like my stories?"

"And then we'll wake up and walk in God knows whatever direction hoping to chance across the little peg-legger's tracks only to, with the fucking help from heaven, track his little cuss mouth down so he can call us all bull dykes again and spit at our faces as we drag him back to his momma who never even says good job at us for our troubles."

"What's wrong with my stories?"

Jilly looked at her. "It's your delivery more than anything else.

Christ, think about who's listening to ya. Would it kill ya to make 'em funny a bit?"

"Nothing's been funny about my whole life."

"Then lie, Mole. Every bitch under the sun has had it hard, but whining about it round a campfire ain't gonna earn you gold stars in the godforsaken afterlife. I pushed my cousin off that roof 'cause he raped my sister, but shit, it just sounds better the other way, and if I tell it the rape way you miss the most important part of it which is the sound he made when he hit the ground."

"You didn't say what sound he made."

"Sometimes it's what you leave out that makes it the best."

Baby Boo tiptoed up with sour eyes.

"Let me fucking guess," Jilly said, "your dumb cunt ass can't light the fucking fire."

Drummond Alone

The poisonous poetry of Drummond's shadow intoxication thinned to whispers as the hours passed. He wasn't quite in focus, but certain things did come to him. Hunger, for instance. His belly felt scratched dry. He tarried from the pond, puked water, and worked his way up the crater wall to the crown of the formation. In the distance, green-leaved trees rolled with the breeze. He went that way, loping confusedly, led on by his hunger.

As he neared, he saw pale-orange fruits that bobbed from the branches.

He picked up speed, reached out and grabbed one. He didn't know it, but they were grapefruit. He bit the rind and bitterness shocked him. The sweet, acidic juice of the thing stung his lips, and he tore open the fruit at the spot he'd bit it, smashed his face into the ruby-red flesh, smeared the sticky thing against his cheeks, nose, and chin. Satisfyingly painful. Burning in some good way.

He made quick work of that one, set to some others, gorged on the grapefruits until his throat stung. The fruits didn't quite quell his hunger, but they dampened it, held it off at some distance to be observed.

He then realized that his skin stung with sunburn. He wished for clothing. He went to lie beneath one of the trees, but there were dropped, dried limbs thick with malicious thorns, and he decided that the area was against him.

He clutched up as many grapefruit as he could gather and retreated to the pond, ambled up over the crater bluff, back down to the water. If he was spotted by those who dwelt on the opposite side from him, he didn't care, wasn't certain.

He made his way back to the cattails and rested again in the mess of them, letting the fruit he'd harvested bob in the water. His haunches sunk into the mud, as did his hands. He lifted a fistful of the stuff, and he figured he'd found an answer. He took the mud and began to run it over his face and shoulders. It was cool against his weathered skin. He smeared his whole body. It felt pleasant. When the sun dried it to a crunchy texture, he washed the earth off him and smeared himself again.

He passed the whole day that way, but the next morning, while hunkering in the reeds, a face gazed toward him from across the pond. He saw it stay on him. A few folks amassed and stayed focused on his position. Drummond threw into anxiety. Queer vibrations beset him. A constriction of his heart transpired.

A few of those across the pond began to round the perimeter of the water toward him. He stepped back, slipped, landed ass down in the mud. The splash must've echoed out. His audience moved toward him with speed—from far away, but he could see.

Drummond plucked his frame from the muck, raced up the

embankment, ran on his bare feet in whatever direction he happened to be moving.

He dashed through tall grasses, low branches, dancing around cacti paddles, their yellow needles catching his thighs, drawing blood. He upped and overed fallen trees, rutted rock formations. Pounced across planes of dirt and pebbles. Hobbled into strands of huizache thorns that pierced the soles of his feet and came out his toes. Anxious, pretend drums thumping some soundtrack for him to escape to.

Tears streaked his face and fear thickened his throat. He never looked back, only raced on. For hours he bolted, moving in some unintentional direction, hoping merely to luck into something to drink, something to eat. Fear and hunger erased the ache of his legs and feet bottoms. Drummond headed east, though he had no idea of his course.

In the gray evening, just before dark, he spotted a quaint house with light in its windows. It rested at the bottom of a slight elevation drop, and he picked up speed as he sank toward it, wild with the idea of being by a fire inside.

"Wait a minute," a woman's voice called from the porch to him.

Drummond slowed, his joy drained. He stood paralyzed, jittery.

"What is ya?"

How long had it been since he spoke? "A Drummond," he answered awkwardly. His jaw tightened, his words sour.

A gun was cocked. A metallic click called out into the pre-dusk. "Don't know what a drummond is."

"I'm naked," said Drummond.

"What's that to me?"

Drummond stood stupid. His eyes bewildered toward nothing. Several moments passed.

"There's a clothesline off there," the woman said, pointing with her gun. She had to motion several times before Drummond noticed. "Get yourself decent off it and come in closer."

Drummond moved that way, found a few things to wrap up in. A shirt that swam on him. Well-worn jeans he had to hold the waist of or they'd slink off.

He went then to the woman who kept the shotgun on him. "You're a filthy thing ain't ya?"

Drummond didn't know, but his face was streaked with mud and he had leaves in his hair.

"Hungry?"

Drummond tried to intimate that he was.

"There's a comet coming," the woman said. "But it won't do nothing to help your kind. And there's no egg pure enough to pluck that dark from your heart. Stay put and I'll get something together, but if you move a muscle I'll shoot you through. My son's one of you, or was last I saw him. I'm sympathetic," the woman said, "but only to a point."

Drummond didn't rightly understand a thing of this. He jittered confusedly, his neck muscles tense. He could hear some banging around taking place in the house.

When she returned, the woman had a pack and some shoes, a length of rope. She held up the sack, spoke loud in Drummond's direction. "In this," she hollered slow, "you'll find some things to eat on. Some biscuits and dried meat. Dried tomatoes. Cheese." She threw the sack out toward him, then held up the shoes. "I don't know your size," she yelped. "And if I did wouldn't matter. This is what I got." She lobbed them out. "I see you're struggling to keep those up, but I can't find a belt." She wrapped the bit of rope up around itself and tossed it out toward Drummond. He picked it off the ground, uncoiled it. His black eyes glanced frantically over it. She motioned around herself, yelled, "Tie it round your waist." And she continued to motion.

Drummond ferreted the rope through the belt holes of his blue jeans, his hands trembling with starvation and shock, and he achieved some awkward knot at the front of himself. He plunged his feet into the shoes easily enough, them being several sizes too big, and he picked up the pack.

"Can you understand me?"

Drummond nodded.

She aimed the gun barrel at him. "I'll count to ten," she said.

Drummond didn't even hear her get to five. He ran until he couldn't.

Then he walked on in his loose shoes, a new kind of confidence to him, for no longer being naked.

After some hours, the air changed. He couldn't quite define it. The world seemed more moist, briny. In the distance, he heard a sort of echo reverberating.

His ears filled with some kind of crashing.

He stood and saw a bit of shadow below him. Paused at the thing. Told himself to leave it alone. Watched it move as he moved. Watched it get nearer to him. Screamed at himself, from somewhere inside to not drink it, but he was closer still. Nothing could be done. He was down on the thing, gulping it up.

He picked up his pack and continued.

The dirt turned to sand beneath him, his steps loose in the softness of it.

He climbed a dune.

If he had once known what the ocean was, that knowledge was lost to him now, and he merely stood in awe at the immensity of it. White waves crashed in rhythms indecipherable and birds ran willy-nilly over the water-packed sand.

He didn't know what to do.

He dropped to his knees.

The noise and the smell engulfed him. Salted static. Brackish hissing.

He gazed out at the infinity of water.

He thought maybe he was in heaven.

He made his way forward.

Waded out.

It warmed his skin. Stung his sores. Pushed him over and dragged him across the sand.

Further.

Deeper.

Further still.

It felt so fucking good his being in it. All the glinting sunlight of the spume and barm about him.

He wanted more of that, it was his now, the whole thing.

He moved out.

Deeper still.

Deep enough that he could taste it.

But even that didn't stop him.

four

The patterns of society's demise played out in different sequences, but in that region, where there was open land to retreat to, dwellings sprung up at the center of vast, forgotten acreages. Families crept off to long-neglected landholdings that had been handed down for generations, to forge life anew in the wake of the world's falling apart. These little tribes of relatives beat their bodies against the earth, dug wells in the old way—with hand shovels over days and days, sending candles down in baskets to check the air for bad gasses—walked plows behind mule power to break up the land into farmable rows. Neo-pioneers, and they existed in the not-too-distant proximity of the falling-away world, watching as fires spat smoke plumes from the dilapidating townships, sitting on stores of fuel and ammunition, arms and provisions accumulated by those fortunate enough to have seen some bad thing coming.

Mostly these holdings of humans clung deep to religious rituals, saw themselves as steadfast refugees the Lord himself had selected to retain his message in, and they'd scrape pews out of tree trunks and sit making new music from old chord changes, taking ancient hymns and retooling their words.

"Be Thou my vision, O Lord of my heart;
Naught be all else to me, save that Thou art;
Thou my best thought, by day or by night;
I won't drink my shadow forged from thy light."

Prophets, seers, revelators: whatever you wanted to call them, they thought themselves that. They let their hair grow wild and clucked bits of scripture at the dizzying enormity of their solitude.

Trains ran. Trains stopped. Trains ran. Trains stopped.

Domes were built and domes were filled. Domes were emptied, domes were filled.

Vast efforts were undertaken, abandoned.

Little wars and tiny treaties.

If they were Christian, they turned to the laws of Leviticus. Never ate rabbits. A single seed. Single fabric.

Muslims held hard to Sharia. No yellow. Untamed eyebrows. No alcohol at all.

Others found meaning in texts non-ordained: "a personal God quaquaquaqua with white beard quaquaquaqua outside time without extension who from the heights of divine apathia divine athambia divine aphasia loves us dearly with some exceptions for reasons unknown but time will tell."

Time told this: there was more time.

Each new unfurling, every coming rapture, all supposed ter-minations—the return of God or the undoing of reality—failed to materialize, and these strange clans begot bizarre progeny who they filled with their insane notions to carry off toward the future.

The Hermit

Let us meet an odd fellow who lives alone, his home fashioned from loose tree limbs he wrestled free from a river's snag, palm fronds slathered with gray clay hoisted out the earth, a sort of grisly hut sunk back in the discarded skeletal remains of animals he'd made meals of. The whole of his denomination lost to him. "Partaking in glory," he'd say of them, their outpost taken by blaze as they slept.

He has a passion for grass fires. His teeth are like oyster gravel. You can smell the funny look in his eyes.

He dawdles the countryside collecting lost bits he might someday find useful, discarded items he feels his destiny will give purpose to, rubbish of note that catches his attention from afar.

He pushes a wheelbarrow across the land, circling his dwelling concentrically, with each pass furthering his circumference, hunting forgotten treasures.

It is on one of these outings he chances upon an elder man with a loose leg over his shoulder, the bloody end of it stuffed into a brown paper bag.

"What you got there?"

The leg-holding man jostled his leg. "A leg."

"For what?"

"Taking it to town for trade."

"What they trade you for it?"

"Things I want, obviously."

He thought about that. "Where's the town at?"

The leg-holding man pointed. "North a ways from here. Not too far off. The Town of Lost Souls."

"Okay," says the hermit, and he pushes his wheelbarrow on, the two going their separate ways.

Much later. Days or weeks. Maybe months even. Our wheelbarrow pusher follows a black-eyed man to the coast. The hermit doesn't know it, but this is Drummond. And he walks about aimless. His clothes don't fit him, and he seems lost. He is sickly. He is low. He strolls across the beach and into the surf and is capsized by waves, tossed by breakers, held down by undertow, and the wheelbarrow pusher stays back, just witnessing.

Ultimately, the body is coughed up by the gulf, spat onto the beach sand, dead to the world.

The wheelbarrow pusher goes to him.

He removes his wet clothes.

"Too big for me," he says, but he keeps them anyway, because maybe he'll grow. He folds them and sets them in his barrow beside a dull hunting knife he recently plucked out of a tree trunk. The notion strikes him. "What could they trade for legs?" He shrugs. He grasps the knife handle, goes to the dead man. He sets into his hips to disjoint the legs, each dull passing of the blade hacking gruesome noise, deep, dark blood spilling to the sand. A horrid clipping of tendons. Leaning his heft to throw the socket out.

When he has each one freed, he hoists Drummond's legs on his load. He smiles at his work. He knows where he's going.

The Town of Lost Souls

The town's history was uncertain, but what it had become was a sort of squatter camp for wastrels and profligates. There existed, on its perimeter, felled and molested signage which reported the population of the place to be 8,231, but that was civilizations ago, and most likely the true number of residents was around one hundred. This odd horde mostly dwelled in a derelict district of brick buildings set along eight streets, four running in each direction, and there seemed a sort of roving order amongst them that fluctuated based on the stages of the moon, which dictated the behavior of the inhabitants. This place, sometimes called The Town of Lost Souls, ran on Darwinian logic, and the only discernible structure to their lives revolved around a machine housed in a park at the town's center. Produced daily from beneath a tarp of canvas, the machine was an abomination of science and nature. Fitted with hoses that ran back to baths of blood, the contraption was little more than a life support that maintained limbs which were fetched back for it. Mostly, the thing housed legs, which dangled from a crossbar that they were fixed to with hooks, tied into the circuitry of the system with hoses that seemed red, but were in actuality see through, filled with blood. These appendages drooped from their housings, live nerves fidgeting meekly. Barefoot, the toenails of them grew yellow and wicked. The wounds, where they'd been hacked from bodies at the thighs and shoulders, were wrapped in gauze that discolored with plasma. A stench of crude antiseptic, iron, and sweat wafted from them. The few arms that were hooked into the device had hands that would open and close at random, the sound of this happening curious and alarming.

Like all things, these limbs aged and had to be replaced at intervals. This degeneration was much faster than the life of normal arms and legs. The oldest leg dangling at any time might have been on the machine two years. For a compensation, the citizenry of the encampment would retrieve new limbs to supplant those that looked on their way out. This exchange for a wage happened intermittently and was handled by a mustached fellow with indurate eyes, who governed over these transactions sternly. He wore a vest with shallow pockets he kept his knuckles tucked into. He had a pencil behind his right ear. He cleared his throat, tongued his teeth. Didn't look folks in the eyes unless they deserved it. They called him Doc, though he never healed anyone.

At the start of the day, a hermit brought him two legs.

"Why'd you bring me both?" Doc asked. The legs had been wrapped in spent fabric that a stiff wind could blow bits off of.

"For trade." There was a spooky character to the leg holder's eyes, a shellfish quality to his teeth.

"This is a fickle beast we got here," Doc said. "What it chooses to support and what it lets die on the hooks is beyond me and I wouldn't tax the thing to take on two of the same risks."

"I don't get it."

"Of course you don't. You're a moron, but I'm a patient man, so allow me to illuminate: some legs don't make it. We hook them up, and then they die." Doc palmed one of the odd man's pilfered legs. "If this leg gets hooked in and dies," he caressed the other, "this one would surely perish as well."

"But if it lives," the stranger quibbled, "there'd be two new legs."

"Do you have a method of ascertaining the chances of that? Are you an actuary in this regard? Is there some math, some data, some figure you could present to me on the matter that would persuade me to chance making a payment for two limbs from the same stock to burden my machine with supporting?"

"I don't . . ."

"Monroe!" said Doc, and a broad figure of a man appeared from behind the machine. "How often do we buy two legs from the same donor?"

"Never." Monroe said.

"Never," said Doc now looking into the man's face. "That's known protocol to those who operate in this camp. But you're new here."

"Been around a bit," the hermit said, but he'd only showed up that morning, straying the streets analyzing the crude society, sort of peeking around corners cautiously. He had seen a pack of wild-shaped men set upon a young boy in some building's entry, strip him of his clothes, chase him naked down the streets, howling at him.

"Been around a bit?" Doc mocked. "I'll give you shadow rights for a week on the one leg, and I'll give you lodging for three day's duration at my inn."

"Shadow rights?"

"I don't haggle," Doc said.

The leg holder didn't know what to make of it, but Doc took his pencil from his ear, marked a card, called out, "Monroe." He gave the marked card to him. "Get this man set up."

Doc was a kind of governor to the entirety of those eight streets. His chief concern was the machine and the maintenance of it and the profit it provided him, the power it gave him over the town. There was no set monetary standard he held allegiance to. He let those who came to sip shadows propose how he'd be compensated. But beyond the trinkets and knickknacks he'd take in trade, he demanded a kind of blind allegiance from his customers. In that encampment he moved and manipulated most endeavors with little more than his expression. Folks watched to see how he took things. They didn't want to be cut off from the machine. Doc's emotions were considered fragile, and everyone wanted to please him. He had the magic quality manipulative people achieve—he could make you feel like you were the true reason air existed, or he could make you feel like your whole life was some misuse of molecules.

As the machine's master, each evening, whether or not all the shadows had been consumed from each limb, he'd order a switch on the thing to be flipped. The blood slowed to a stall. The limbs wriggled and fidgeted, kicked and punched. When they were all still, essentially dead, the switch was thrown again. The blood flowed. The limbs reanimated. The process brought their shadows back to them.

They were ready for the next day.

Unlucky Clover

The jail in The Town of Lost Souls was most likely antiquated before shadow addiction spoiled the world. It probably didn't function in any capacity beyond lending a kind of curiosity to those who ventured to visit it—a museum of sorts that people would tour so as to see how criminals used to be treated. In its current incarnation it served as a makeshift depository for Doc's goods. There were two cells, both in use but for severely different reasons. In one cell, Doc kept the things he considered dear: gold artifacts perchance, taxidermied species of note, weaponry of forgotten civilizations. In the other cell, he kept Joe Clover. It was out of spite he kept him.

In that cell, no sunlight shone. The misery this brought Clover set him about to whine and wallow. He had naught but his nudity to keep him entertained, and he wanted his shadow the way babies want warmth.

From the streets you could hear him moaning piteously. Because of this, they called him Unlucky Clover, and Doc made certain his presence was known. Clover was the only man who'd ever tried to upset Doc's proprietorship of the machine, and Doc used Clover's punishment as a cautionary tale to any who might chance something so stupid again.

Clover'd been held captive for weeks. When he first came in, he had hair down past his ass, but after a day or so in his cell, he'd made to hang himself with a rope he fashioned from the stuff— opting for death rather than a forced sobriety.

They found him dangling, near blue, and Doc had his minions hack his hair off to prevent another such attempt. They kept his cell empty, Joe Clover naked. His sloppy-butchered hair made him look like an overgrown orphan.

Doc liked to come in and watch Clover sulk. Liked to see him gross in his cage. He'd look down at the wreckage and chide him. "Sorensen says when you lift a rock, you do not find a preexisting shadow."

"Who the fuck is Sorensen?"

"Roy Sorensen. A shadow expert before all this went down. My father's favorite writer. A philosopher and great thinker, the antithesis of you."

"How long you gonna hold me?"

"Indefinitely."

Clover had tried to starve himself to death but wasn't strong enough a person. Doc had brought him steak and potatoes. The steak was cut before it was passed in, wrapped in paper. He gave him a plastic cup of grapefruit moonshine.

"What did you even think would happen?" Doc asked.

Clover's hair was freshly butchered and he was a bit loose on grapefruit moonshine. "Fuck you mean think would happen?"

"Do you remember any of it? Leading up to the cage?"

The smell of rust from the bars of the jail cell. The blight smell of moonshine. The smell of stagnant water from Clover's commode. Clover's mind filled with grainy thoughts and dissolving half recollections. If he thought too long on any memory, it crumbled. He faintly flashbacked to pushing Doc down from behind. "It doesn't matter."

"It doesn't?" Doc looked around at the jail.

Clover sipped his moonshine. "Give me some more of this." He drained his cup, handed it to Doc.

"Sure," said Doc. He took the empty cup from Clover and tossed it to the ground. "Soon as hell turns to pudding pie."

"Asshole."

"You know how many shadows a person has?" Doc spoke at Clover as though addressing excrement.

Clover eyed the ground where his false-light shadow lay. "Depends."

"No it doesn't" said Doc. "You have exactly none. Sometimes you cast a shadow, but Sorensen says a hole made by an object is never part of that object. See, light travels in straight lines. Do you know why you're in a cage?"

"Sure," said Clover, "it's because you're a crazy shithead."

"Nope," said Doc, "my mental state's beside the point." He stuck a hand through the jail bars, sort of waved it. "It's because of this here space between the bars. Otherwise, you'd be in a box."

"Hysterical."

"Suck the space out."

"What?"

"From the cage," said Doc. "Suck it out. Make it a box."

Clover grimaced. He brushed against the jail bars. Rusty iron things, textured like tree limbs, nearly. "Can't be done, fucker."

Doc held up a finger. "I'm inclined to agree with you, except I've seen you do such a thing. No one *has* a shadow. People *cast* shadows. That is to say, your shape cuts a hole in the light. Drops darkness on some terminus in the approximation of your figure."

"Shadows ain't holes, dipshit."

"They most certainly are. Absences of light. The way flute holes are absences of flute. We've just given them a name. You ever hear of a transplant?"

"A what?"

"For amputees? Before the world turned to shit, they could do it. Take an arm from one person, put it on another. Or a leg. Or a finger."

"You been in the sun too long dinking with your machine. You've lost your mind."

"How would one go about that? Losing your mind? You can't cut the thing off me. You can't transplant it like an arm."

"You ain't even making sense."

"If we took your arm, and put it on my body, would I be guilty for all the wrongs you did with that arm?"

"What?"

"If somehow your mind took sanctuary in my skull, would it be a sin to execute my body on account of the crimes your mind did prior?"

Clover closed his eyes.

"What part of us makes *us* us?" Doc asked. "The arms and legs out there? On my machine. With the right tools, I could make them anybody. Are they only objects then? Like hats or pants?"

Joe Clover grabbed his junk. "If you ever get done talking," he said, "feel free to suck my dick." He wallowed off to a corner of his cell.

"Guess I'm done," said Doc. "But if your dick ever ends up in my mouth, I'll make it an object to suck shadow from. I'll dangle it from my machine."

The Trip toward Town

The night before they left, Mira had a look at Bale's feet. He had his boots kicked off, sat back in a recliner. She stood in front of him, cradled a foot against her waist. The soles of the things were sullen black, direful. "I don't know how you can stand to walk around like this."

Bale lifted his chin, refined his gaze on her. "Must be all the years of dish washing."

Mira set the one foot down, lifted the other. "You're kidding, right?"

"Oh no," Bale said, "it's a tough gig."

Murk rubbed his stump. "I fucking hate washing dishes."

Bale leaned forward toward Murk, the crown of his Mohawk aimed at him. "I'd wash for ten hours every day. They'd come in in cartfuls. Bowls and spoons we ate rations off of. They kept the wash water so hot it made your hands fall apart." He opened a palm toward Mira and she touched it. "Feels like shit, right?"

She shook her head.

"Out here's been the easiest my life has ever been. Which is funny because back in school they made soldiers sound like immortal things. All you do is stand around pointing a gun at shit. Washing dishes takes a hero by comparison. Even hauling the tracks. No big deal. It's all easy compared to dish washing."

"All of it's easy?" Mira said.

"Sure. The walk to town will be nothing. How far is it anyhow?"

"It'll take a day and some."

"Will your mom be all right alone that long?"

"Gotta be," said Mira. "I'll do something I haven't done in a while."

IN THE MORNING, Mira led a goat from its pen and into the sun. She whispered some words at it, apologies mostly. She knew the thing was dying regardless—eventually it would be food. Mira would bind its hind legs and run a knife across its jugular, hang it from a tree branch above a bowl to catch its blood. Something in this, though, felt darker. It was a fouler molestation, perhaps akin to rape. The taking of a thing's shadow was felt in a different and dirty way. Animals seemed embarrassed by it. Afterwards, they'd trot off—or amble in whatever manner they maneuvered in—and look at Mira accusingly. They'd seem spooked, badgered.

In her whispering way, once it was done, she'd apologize again. It was the case with this nanny kid. She arched her back and bucked off a ways.

It did hurt, the thing said.

Hurt? said Mira, of course none of this actually with words.

Maybe not quite.

Mira led the thing back to its pen, walked into where her mother sat, huddled in her agony, oddly draped in dark. Mira lowered to her, breathed into her lips. Once swallowed, her mother gave her an odd expression, but then she was asleep.

THEY PACKED FOOD and water, some blankets and matches. Bale made to bring his rifle.

"I like where your head's at," said Murk. "But that thing would give us away. Not many people have those out here. We show up to town with it, every eye will be on us. I don't know the exact numbers, but I'd say there's at least a hundred there. Even if those are magic, five-people-killing bullets there'll be plenty of folks leftover pissed 'bout what we done to their friends. So, we leave it here, it don't help us at all, but we bring it and it don't help us enough for the attention it calls to us."

Bale patted his rifle, reluctantly set it aside.

THEY WALKED FOR hours. They had divvied up the weight of their provisions, sharing the load.

"Did we bring a rope?" Murk asked.

"No one's fucking flying you," Mira said.

ON AND ON they went—the slow steps and the drudged task of taking them.

"Back in the dome," Bale said, "I would've killed to get to walk this much."

"Now?"

"I'd kill to get carried."

"Wanna piggy back?" Mira asked.

"Serious?"

"Of course not."

• • •

A DEER RAN across the glade.

"Did y'all have pets at all?"

"We had some stuff in aquariums we could go look at. Aside from that, there were roaches and rats and things like that. Cats that didn't really belong to anyone. Geckos. I tried to keep one of those once but I tore off his tail holding it and then looking at the thing just made me feel bad."

"What'd you do with it after that?" Murk asked.

"Put it in the trash. I think."

"So you all took showers together?"

"Pretty much."

"Boys and girls same time?" Mira asked.

"Nah. They split us up."

"And you'd just be together all the time? Must be weird being with that many people who've seen you naked."

"I've seen you naked," said Murk.

"When?"

"When I did."

"Recent?"

"Recent enough that you had titties and kitty feathers."

"Well you don't count anyhow, and you're just one. If it was hundreds, that'd be a different thing."

"It was thousands," said Bale.

"But what if you get hurt real bad?" said Bale.

"Like worse than this?" Murk raised his peg.

"We saw a doctor every week," Bale said. "Even if we weren't sick. Poked us with needles and things. Took our blood. I once saw a lady brought back from the dead."

"When I was young," said Mira, "this lady used to come around every so often and she had things in bottles you could trade for. She said they did different things to heal you, but pretty much they just made you feel like you were floating and made your teeth loud."

"Teeth loud?"

"When you clicked them," she said.

"You got some shadow back," Bale said to Murk.

Murk stopped. He had a faint shadow emerging. He squatted and sipped it gone. He stood, clicked his teeth. "Loud as shit," he said, "and that was free."

"So at the edge of your shadow," said Murk, "it, like, glows."

Bale considered it. They walked along. "Yeah kinda."

"And, it's like," Murk rubbed his chin, "everything it passes over, as we're walking and all, seems to bend. Like time travel."

"Um . . ."

"And . . ."

"You should quit looking at it."

They came to a cluster of mesquite trees parked at the base of a bluff.

"It's as good a place as any to camp, I'd guess," said Murk.

They dropped their bags near a tree trunk, walked through the coppice hunting dismissed limbs that had been lost long enough ago that they'd gone dry in the heat of days. They amassed a bundle and scratched together kindling, twig bits and dry grass.

They rallied together a sort of camp that way—built a fire at the edge of the trees, laid out blankets to bed on.

Mira had a Dutch oven she set in the flames, warmed goat stew for them to dine on. They ate from earthen mugs with wooden spoons. They passed the canteen back and forth.

"There's one thing I miss for certain," said Bale.

"What's that?"

"Climate control. It was always the perfect temperature in the dome."

The sky grew dim as night approached.

"Y'all tell ghost stories in the Dome?" Murk asked.

"Kind of," said Bale.

Mira got excited, sat forward, kind of clapped her hands. "Tell one."

"Hell, I'll probably mess it up."

"We won't know," Murk said. "If it's bad, we'll just blame dome people in general. We'll pretend it had nothing to do with you."

Bale thought a minute. "Okay," he said, "here's the best one I know."

The Miserable Mother

"When my people first moved into the dome it split families apart. Not everyone wanted to go. There was a young woman who was married to a shadow sipper, and they had a son. She loved the boy more than anything on Earth, but when she told the shadow-sipping father she was moving into the dome, he told her she could go but that the boy was staying in the outside world. It broke the woman's heart. She didn't want to stay in the sun, but she didn't want to leave her boy either. He had crystal blue eyes, and she loved to look at them. In the end, she decided she couldn't leave him. She watched the rest of her family board the train that led to the dome, and she watched the world around her thin out of good folks and get filled up with bad.

"She did her best to raise her child, but, as the years passed, it became harder and harder to provide for him. The husband wasn't any help. He didn't hunt or farm. He didn't keep house or teach the boy.

"One day, the women went off looking for food—all their cupboards were bare. When she got back, her son and husband were in the front yard together. It seemed suspicious. She called her boy, and he went to her.

"She knelt down to look at his eyes, and they were black as eight balls."

"Y'all got pool tables in there?" Murk asked.

"Yeah, you play?"

"Couple times. I was good at it."

"Bet I'd beat you . . ."

Mira kicked at Bale, "Finish the damn story."

"Right," said Bale. "So she saw his eyes.

"And then she realized she'd made a great mistake. The rest of her family was safe in the dome, and she'd stayed out in the world to take care of a boy now lost to her. It broke her heart, but she decided maybe there was still hope.

"She ran to the train tracks and followed them in the direction her family had traveled off in. It took her days, but she finally got to the dome.

"It was completely shut up, but she walked the outskirts of it, banging the walls. The only family she still knew was inside it. All that was outside and with her had changed beyond her knowing.

"She went insane.

"Her last days were spent aiming to get inside the dome.

"She banged the walls. She attempted tunneling in.

"Ultimately, she died that way. Out there, going crazy.

"When death came, she welcomed it. She slumped against the dome, and breathed her final breaths, happy that her pain and suffering was over.

"But she was wrong.

"When her body died, her soul stepped from it, and as soon

as it saw the dome, it latched on to the idea that it could now, without the body limiting it, gain entry easily.

"But the soul could not.

"The rules that governed the woman in life governed her in death as well.

"And so at night, you could hear her. Against the roofs and the walls, scratching and banging.

"And she'd have to go on that way forever."

"Not bad," said Murk.

"Works better back home," said Bale, "'cause you can usually hear banging and such."

"Think it's her?"

"I think it's somebody."

The night was still. Filled with the music of the fire and insects chirping. Owls hooted. Coyotes howled.

Murk, Bale, and Mira laid back in their blankets. Pretty soon, they were all asleep.

The Women in Darkness

Not far off, Jilly and Mole sat in darkness and, just beyond, Baby Boo rubbed sticks trying to get a fire going.

"Stupid bitch," said Jilly. "Just let me make the goddamn fire."

"If we coddle her she'll never learn."

"I don't give a fuck if she learns. I don't care if her brain falls out her asshole. I'm cold and it's dark and I wanna sleep."

"Think about something else."

"Like what?"

"I got a story," Mole said.

Jilly covered her eyes with her hand. "Oh thank all the gods above. Thank the stars that twinkle and the moon that glows too."

"It's a good one. Been working on it."

Jilly lowered her hand, her face angry. She motioned to Mole with a flippant gesture. "Regale us," she said. "Hesitate not to enamor our minds with the narrative you've been a cooking up."

Mole cleared her throat, adjusted her repose. "My uncle had a little dick," she said, "and it had a funny flavor."

Nothing spoke but the night.

Jilly looked around her, side to side. "Am I in some kind of nightmare?"

"Didn't like it?"

"How the hell is that a story? Ain't nothing even to it."

"I was leaving things out, like you said. To make it funny."

Jilly blinked many times. "How the hell could that be funny? You sucked your uncle's tiny dick? Fucking hysterical. Does it feel better to get that out? 'Cause I tell you, I'm not much for talking feelings. I feel like sharing shit like that just drags others down. You got a memory like that, you let that shit fester. Keep that poison in you and just learn to move on."

"I didn't say I sucked it," Mole said.

"Come again?"

"He hanged himself. In winter. Mom and I found him and figured he shouldn't go to waste. We cut him down from his tree branch and cooked him up, and I asked mom what dick tasted like, and she didn't know so we tossed it in the frying pan a bit and chewed on it some, but it was nasty so I spit my bite in the fire."

Baby Boo looked up from her fire starting.

Mole seemed proud of herself.

Jilly made to speak, but, for the first time since her year of silence, she couldn't think of a thing to say.

The Inn

Everything deplorable in that world drained toward the inn at the Town of Lost Souls. Riffraff amassed there in the nights to freely congregate in debauchery. Black-eyed drifters, grim-faced ladies with skirts freely hiked. Each customer foul toothed, speaking slurred profanities. The heavy scent of sandalwood incense, bathtub alcohol, stale tobacco smoke, bodily fluids. Macabre tunes hovered in this fluky bouquet, banged out on an out-of-tune pianola by a one-eyed midget who lowed abridged lyrics seemingly unintended for his audience—hooligans who tarried and bungled their ways about the first-floor saloon of the joint. Upstairs, the doors of a dozen lodging rooms lined a banistered walkway, the banister leading to a staircase that descended against the back wall. In the far front of the inn, on the lower level, a ragged pool table stood, and men lingered about it holding cues, their eyes blinking involuntarily whenever the balls struck each other. Glasses were set on the copper bar, clinked together. Doors were opened and closed. Men and women called harassments at each other. Occasionally, wild fucking could be heard from above.

In his room, sitting on the floor with his back to the door, clutching the leg that could not be traded, the hermit's wild eyes seemed even wilder. He could feel the sin of that scene against him, could taste the dereliction in the air.

Terrified, he resigned to sleep in his current position, making it less possible that he might be molested in the night.

The bed in his room stayed made. He wouldn't touch it. He feared it had been soaked through with bad deeds that would most likely bring him nightmares or gift his skin with some communicable irritation.

He whispered some half-remembered prayers to himself.

He tried not to listen to the noise of all the bad deeds around him.

The smell of the putrid leg clutched to him—aroma so blubbery you could mark it with teeth.

Downstairs, a young boy was dragged into the madness of the saloon by his hair, tossed onto the pool table and held down to it.

The leader of this enterprise addressed the crowd. He seemed liked a disheveled clergyman from some religion that worshipped motor oil. "This boy here is the son of my brother, but I will not call him nephew yet. His father is long lost to us, and his mother is buried and I have grown tired of his irksome ways."

The boy struggled with his restrainers. Flopped about on the felt. Spat where he could spit.

"He is, however, the only family I have, and we are aiming now to tame him some." The uncle pulled a bowie knife from his belt. "I apologize for the noise, but we've no other place to perform the procedure."

Some madnesses are so bizarre that they entice witnessing.

Those in the bar who had been preoccupied with debauchery, who had been lost in the melee of drinking and lustful deeds, tapered their pursuits in order to watch this odious operation. Even the bartender waved off those waiting for drinks, came out from his station with a bottle in each hand and took up closer to the pool table, pouring willy-nilly shots out for his patrons nearest him, spilling here and there, as his attention was on the nephew now writhing with all his might.

The uncle laid his hand upon the boy's chest, bulldozed his body down, the thump of it sending shockwaves through the floor, rattling feet. "I'll give you the choice, a luxury, when you think on it right."

"Fuck off," rumbled the boy. His smooth face streaked with tears, his mouth puckered, lips quivering.

"Not yet," said the uncle. "Arm or leg?" He raised up from the boy, tested the sharpness of his knife blade with the pad of his thumb, awaited the answer. But no answer came. The uncle cleared his throat. "Choose or I'll choose for you." He tapped the light that dangled above the pool table. His face was marred with scars that must've been made by human fingernails. His eyes twinkled hideously. "Arm or leg?"

Now the audience participated. "Leg," screamed one, "hooks don't work for shit." He raised his right arm, and the hook on the end of it gleamed.

"You ever walk on a peg, dumb fucker?" hollered some other patron. "Give him the arm you use least, I say."

Then there was a sort of blathering of opinions. A cacophony of suggestions. Expert testimony as to which limb to choose.

Simple stories about hindrances that would emerge either way. Proclamations as to how no matter what, he'd get used to it.

"Neither's so bad," said some spooky woman. She was missing her left leg. She was missing her right arm. She only had two teeth in her mouth and she licked at them wickedly as though trying to make them clean with her tongue.

The uncle shook his head, a perturbed mien in his eyes. "I'll give you ten seconds," he said, stepping up closer to the boy. "Nine."

"Don't make me choose neither," the boy said, bucking. "I'll be perfect from now on. I swear it. I'll do as you say."

"Eight."

Chants came up from the crowd. "Leg. Leg. Leg."

And in opposition. "Arm. Arm. Arm."

Louder now, the uncle, as though to some god or magistrate or arbiter or czar, "Seven."

"Leg. Leg."

"Six."

"Arm. Arm."

"Five."

All the heaving preposterous stenches of breath and adrenaline and shock and dismay. All the stale light and dirty glasses with drops of moonshine in them quavering with the impromptu ceremony.

"Four."

"Let me keep 'em both. Daddy wouldn't want it like this." The boy heaved this way and that. Wriggling and floundering and tussling and strife in his eyes. Every vein preached forward behind his skin as though he'd burst open in some seismic rupture, spew out of himself like a tidal wave and wash against those who crowded him.

"Three. Daddy's dead or doesn't care else he'd be here."

"Leg. Leg."

"Arm. Arm."

And the one impartial woman with her wild open mouth licking her two teeth furiously, a kind of fucked-up glee in her eyes.

"Two." And the uncle set into the boy, his arm oscillating, so his bowie knife dangled now over the shoulder, then over the hip. The shoulder.

"Arm. Arm."

The hip.

"Leg. Leg."

"One," said the Uncle.

"Wait, wait," said the boy.

A great silence fell. The labored breathing of the held-down boy.

The knife. Above the shoulder. Above the hip. The stillness of the waiting crowd. All things pitched up to nothing. Like some arrow shot straight in the air that pauses, briefly, before gravity calls it home.

A voice came from the shadows, "Sorensen says that hearing silence is a successful perception of an absence of sound."

"The fuck?" said the uncle.

"And that pauses depend on sounds just as the hole of a doughnut depends on the doughnut."

"Who the hell is that?"

Doc stepped forward. "The boss," he said. All eyes averted

then. To be able to see it as Doc saw it. The quick flick of the gaze of all present toward the ground. Obedience in gesture form. "I thought I'd weigh in." Doc went then to the edge of the table. "I got a leg just this morning for the machine. So, I say we take an arm, keep things even."

The arm faction cheered.

The boy struggled. "Which one you use least?" Doc asked. He patted the boy's brow. Gazed into his eyes. Bowed his head a bit, showing pity.

"No, sir, please. You can help me, I know it," said the boy.

"Look at these people, son. You can tell from their eyes. It's going to happen. You can't change minds when they're this certain of what they want. It's important you answer. And answer me true: which arm do you use the least?"

The boy struggled some more. Thrashed in his captors' grips. But he was spent. "My left," he said, his black eyes rimmed so deeply red they looked as though they might launch from his face like rockets.

"You sure?" said Doc.

"Yes."

"Think it through," said Doc. "All the tasks you do. You use your right arm the most? Opening doors? Wiping your ass?"

"I'm sure," the boy said. "I'm right-handed. I barely even use the left one for anything I don't guess."

"Good," said Doc. "So long as you're sure."

"I'm certain. I'm certain." He nodded as much as his restrainers allowed him. "Right-handed all my life."

Doc beheld the uncle, the nephew. "Not anymore you're not. Give me his right arm."

"Wait. I was lying. I was lying."

The crowd erupted. Guttural hymns the color of nightmares. Sound so thick you could eat it off a cracker.

"It'll be a good lesson for you," Doc said. "Don't ever let anyone choose for you."

"Fucking no," the nephew gasped. "Uncle, take the left. Uncle."

Doc motioned for it to begin, and the uncle swiped the massive bowie blade across the right shoulder's flesh, and the thing drained open, the pool-table felt guzzling up the oozing blood, and the stain crawling out around the boy the way universes expand.

The shrieking then. The wild bemoaning of the boy and the euphoric cheering of the crowd that heaved forward into the table's frame and formed some thick audience, roaring with jubilation as the boy's favorite arm was hacked from him.

Upstairs, in his room, the hermit heard the bloodcurdling gasp of a child in distress. He clutched his foul-stenched, severed leg to his body like a baby with a blanket.

Morning

Mira, Murk, and Bale woke dew glazed. Their fire was down to hot ashes. Mira stirred them, threw in some kindling. Smoke fussed toward the sky. She had corn batter in a container that she poured into her Dutch oven and set it in the coals. She sat over the vessel, watching their breakfast cook. Bale and Murk packed up and Mira divvied up hunks of hot bread onto pieces of parchment that she passed to the boys, and they sat and ate in silence, the early morning quiet. Only a few birds cooed.

"We'll leave the Dutch oven here. It's too hot to carry and we should be back this way."

"Should?" There was corn pone in Murk's teeth.

"Well, hopefully not you."

Murk fingered out the pone, said, "You'll regret that if it's true."

"How much farther is it?" Bale asked.

"A few hours. We might could've walked all the way last night, but we'd've gotten there dead tired."

Bale stretched and yawned. "I'm dead tired right now."

When they were all packed up, and about to make way, they heard voices from the trees. Bickering of sorts. Cuss words.

Later, Bale would say he thought for certain they were about to die.

Morning at the Inn

When light touched the window of his room, our leg holder sagged awake. He sniffed a bit, the turning stench of leg thick about him, and he stood, letting the thing fall away from his grip. Flies buzzed about. Elsewhere in the inn, the faint grumbling of others' affairs—vomitus hacking and grousing and rustling. He arranged himself as well as he was able, clutched up his leg and exited the room.

Descending the stairs, his eyes awed at the catastrophe. Broken chairs and busted bottles. Limp humans strewn much like fallen cushions. Passed out or dead, he wasn't certain. Behind the bar, a young boy sloshed a rag in a bucket of gray water, plucked it out and wrung it near dry before wiping the surfaces around him.

"Is it like this every morning?"

"Nah," the boy said, wiping. "Usually worse."

The hermit left the inn, moved through the town with reservation. He wanted to head home, but he felt the need to unload this second leg first.

He stopped a grubby woman who busied herself setting out

trinkets to sell. She had a cart that she worked from, but he couldn't see common traits to the things she sold. There were lightbulbs and pocketknives and eyeglasses and measuring cups, so perhaps she was kindred to him somehow, and he wondered about his own diversified possessions back home, and he wished he had them so he could set up a stand to rival her own. "Think there'd be a market for this?" He showed her the leg.

"Dear God," she said. "It's too turned for the machine."

"Tried the machine yesterday, but they didn't want it."

"Well," she polished up some of her wares, "I can't think a use for it beyond that, but who knows, you might get lucky."

The streets were ghost-town run down, morning-after ill. "When's the town get going?"

"When it does," the woman said.

The hermit walked the lonely place, his only company the rotting leg's foulness.

Suggestion

Jilly and Mole deliberated while Baby Boo kept Murk, Bale, and Mira at gunpoint.

"I mean," said Jilly, "if he's behind a train, we kill him. If he's running away from a train we're attacking, we kill him."

"Yeah, but if they throw him out. Is he technically still a domer?"

"If that little redheaded fucker did what he was told, we wouldn't even have to deal with this shit."

"When we find him, I'm gonna ask for a different position."

Murk, Mira, and Bale communicated with their eyes and Murk made to change the topic. "How long ago he go missing? This redhead? Maybe we can help."

"None your fucking business," said Jilly.

"Y'all try the town?"

"I ain't going to that rat-shit place to hobnob with miscreants like you. That boy went there he can stay there as far as I'm concerned."

208 BRIAN ALLEN CARR

"We could go look for you." Murk wriggled a bit where he sat. "We're headed that way."

Baby Boo put the barrel of her rifle against Murk's forehead.

"Just a suggestion." Murk backed off it all.

The breakfast fire crackled and some dark sense of anticipation seemed tethered to its crackling. A notion of doom in the wood's turning to embers.

"Wait, there might be something to that," said Mole. "I mean, the town's probably filled with his kind of people. Scum draws scum to scum. Usually."

"Sure," said Jilly, "but we just gonna let 'em waltz off with nothing but our trust to guide their way."

"We wouldn't just be trusting them," Mole said.

Into Town

"We shouldn't've left him." Mira said.

"I don't know we had a choice."

"Murk, what the hell are we doing?" She scanned his burnt-looking eyes.

"Going to find Clover. Going to town."

"And then? Who knows what they'll do to Bale when we come back empty-handed."

They moved from the brush into a field of sun-destroyed grass, the blades of it near ossified and yellow as plaque—a crunchy carpet of lifeless growth. Hundreds of yards off, the town stood. A shabby thing that sprang from charred buildings which slunk with decay, and graffitied walls stood lonesome and untethered. Here and there, roofs from old houses sat leveled on the ground. Telephone poles like ancient tombstones cocked this way and that in gangly fashion. A putrid reek of long-dead something.

Murk snorted a deep breath of it. "Yeah, it's a half-baked agenda we got, but what are the options? You said yourself the comet's coming soon, so if this does work we gotta find out fast."

"Maybe we should just make camp a day, go back and say we didn't see him. Just see what transpires."

"And not even try?" They both stood still, disregarding the town. "That would be a waste of so many steps. It's fear you got."

"Probably."

Murk patted her shoulder. "I'll go. You wait for me."

"Really? Think that would be better? Just me? Here? Alone?"

Murk studied the area. "Yeah, probably not."

"Give me a second," Mira said.

Murk kneeled, drank what shadow he had.

"When I say leave we leave."

"Of course," said Murk.

"And I want a kind of password."

"Password?"

"Or a signal. Something only you know. So if I say it or do it, we're out."

"Name it."

Mira thought. "A world with two suns," she said. "I say that, and we go."

"I like it," said Murk. "You could sing it, even."

"Fuck that," said Mira. "I ain't singing your song."

Then they made their way through the wasting field.

Bale with the Women

"You said they had to come back by tomorrow," Bale said. "But what time tomorrow? Sunrise? Noon?"

"You don't need to know that," Jilly said.

Bale fought against his restraints a bit. "But I mean, if you're gonna shoot me, it'd be nice to know how much time I'm looking at."

Jilly had revulsion in her eyes. "You think most people know when they're gonna die? You think that's a convenience the Lord should give us? That we are eternally aware of the events leading up to our perishing? Given some sort of parameters by which to verify the coming of our demise? You think Mole and I should lay that out for you? That we should bless you with an understanding of your death beyond that which most receive? Because I assure you most people's death comes as an absolute shock to them. Comes in the night while they sleep or from the brilliant who knows where in the form of a bullet. Strikes them down while they are deep in a state of unawares and doesn't even give them time enough to make a brief amends to God or whoever they love, and they might die with sin in their mouths and hate in their soul. But we should treat you better? Why? So you can get right with whatever dome deity you swear to, lay it all out bare to them. Profess your sorrow internally that your lord might forgive all your malfeasances? Nope. I've known better people than you who never got that luxury, and I'll be damned if I'm gonna do better by you than them. Why would you even deserve that?"

Bale clicked his pretty teeth. "Just making small talk, I guess."

Mole kneeled in the dirt. Mole tended the fire.

Meeting Doc

When they entered the town, folks looked up from their doings with suspicious eyes. A single wanderer, upon entering that township, might go relatively unnoticed, but for there to be two strangers emerging into the dawdling street seemed oddball, a near insurrection brewing.

Whispers flittered, shoulders were touched. Folks went telling other folks, the way the curious do. "Come look," they'd say to one another, and this curiosity was not lost on Mira and Murk.

"I think it's you that's drawing their attention," said Mira.

"Shit, I might as well have been born on this street. Bet they all think they've seen me before." Murk waved at one of the whisperers. Said simply, "Howdy."

The man he spoke at was a gritty little beast, his rat features tense and nervous, a coating on him like chalk dust. "The hell y'all from?" he asked, shooing toward Murk. He stood askance on a wooden walkway, a creaking sound coming from his footing as he gestured.

"Around," Murk said.

From far enough away, perhaps there was an order to it, but slunk into the trimmings of it, the town was a chaotic contraption. Every action seemed accident driven.

They turned up a street and were met by a small crowd carrying clubs. The man in front pointed at Murk, "You're a peg legger," he said.

"Mighty astute of you," said Murk.

"Y'all gonna have to come with me."

"That's a bit forward, ain't it? I don't even know your name."

"It's Monroe," Monroe said.

"That don't fit our plans."

"Adjust them then. Or we can adjust them for you."

Mira quickly counted about a dozen men clutching some manner of crude weaponry. "It's okay," she said. "We can make time for you."

MONROE LED THEM through the belch-scented streets, in and out of catastrophic herds of black-eyed drudgers—limp and staggering, a dirge in the noise of their lowly to and fro. They worked their way to Doc and his machine, and Doc sat on his stool—the humble throne he held dominion from. "I like your jacket," Doc said. He shook hands with Murk and Mira. "What brings you?"

"To town?" Murk said. "Our steps. To you?" he continued. "These people."

"Monroe," Doc said, "go relax somewhere."

"Close by, Doc?"

"Close enough." Doc had Murk and Mira follow him toward the machine. "Folks like you sometimes come to town for vengeance or something, so I intercept the legless and armless as they enter, bring 'em over to ascertain their intentions. Your leg's not here."

"I'm not looking for it."

"But you're looking for something."

"Just somebody," Mira said. "It's not important."

Doc pocketed his knuckles, leaned back a bit. "Well, if they're here, I know it. Not much happens in this town I don't know. Your eyes aren't black."

"Neither are yours."

Doc fondled one of the hands that dangled from the machine. He fingered its fingers, and the hand seemed to pull away slightly, ball into a fist. "Never had the notion. Who is it you're after?"

"I'd rather not say." The hands on the machine squirmed somewhat.

"No harm in looking for someone."

"Listen," said Mira. "We don't want to end up on your machine."

"I don't put whole people up there. Sorensen asks: When we shake hands, do our shadows become one?"

"Excuse me?"

"We can shake on it. Tell me who you're after, and I'll promise you won't end up on my machine. I'm curious is the thing. You have my attention."

Mira and Murk communed with their eyes.

"Well?" said Doc.

Mira stepped toward Doc, held out her hand. The two shook, but, on the earth, where Doc's shadow fell, it was as if he shook hands with nothing.

"Joe Clover," Mira said.

Doc chuckled at the sky, called out, "Monroe, they've come to town to find Clover." And Monroe's men broke into hoopla, some of them rolling—an over-exaggerated bemusement at the notion.

"I don't get it," said Mira.

"See this leg here," Doc took up a leg, its flesh discoloring. "This came to me yesterday, and it's not gonna take. You can tell right?" he ran the back of his finger down the limb. "Just looks unhealthy." Doc grabbed the leg and snapped it from its housing and blood drooled off the end of it. "I pull 'em once I can tell." He tossed it away to the dirt. "It'd be too hard on my machine to leave it up there decaying, and Joe Clover was kind of like that. A thing that was turning." Doc caressed a few more feet, just sort of slightly touching the heels. "Y'all come with me," he said.

Mira and Murk followed to a building's door. A sign on the wall said JAIL HOUSE.

"What's in there?" asked Mira.

Doc beamed at the sign. "What you're after."

The smell of the place was noxious. Moist, human odors and rust.

They heard stirring before their eyes adjusted to the dim light.

"Who's with you?" a voice asked.

"Visitors," said Doc.

"I don't know 'em."

"Well they know you."

"I like the look of the one. She a gift?" Clover stood there naked, started pawing his cock.

"Knock it off," said Doc.

"Wanna be my creature?" he asked Mira.

"I'll call in Monroe."

"Oh, c'mon, Doc," he said, "Just put her against the bars." His voice raspy with lust.

"Monroe!" hollered Doc, and Monroe came in, his eyes alert. "Restrain him," Doc said pointing at Clover, and Monroe opened the cage, thumped Clover a few times with his fists, drove him to the ground and pulled an arm behind his back.

"Fucking Monroe prick," Clover hollered. "Put her in here, Doc. Just a little favor." Clover leered up at Mira with his butchered hair and sickened eyes, and he grinded against the floor, sort of whispering, "Creature," up at her.

"Well," said Doc, "hope y'all didn't come far. That is about what he has to offer."

The sound of Clover's struggle, his *creaturing*.

"Mind if I kill him?" said Murk. There seemed no sense in lying.

"I figured anybody looking for Clover would want to, but, no, I can't let it happen. Don't get me wrong, he deserves it. Probably deserves a million different deaths for a million different reasons, but as of now he is dying a death he deserves for tampering with me, and the death I have chosen for him is a prolonged one."

Clover's face twitched, he gritted teeth, screeched, "Creature." And Monroe thumped the back of his head a few times, and one shot must've got him good, because he quit fucking the floor, quit whispering *creature*.

Inside the small prison, that last bit of struggle reverberated. Somewhere, water slurped into a foul-smelling drain.

"There's no sun in here," said Murk.

"No sun, no joy, no laughter. Not for Clover."

Monroe got up, stepped out of the cell, turned and locked it.

Silence owned the room.

Mira watched Clover hunkered in his nakedness, his skin gray with filth. She looked to the other cell, brimming with treasures. "What's all that?"

"My things," Doc told her. "Stuff I like."

Mira's mouth hung open. Murk just shifted weight.

"It's not how you wanted it to go. I can tell just by looking, but it doesn't have to be all bad. Stay. Enjoy yourself. Have a drink at the bar on me. You'll be safe your whole stay, and that's a better deal than most visitors get." He put his thumbs in his vest pockets. "I mean, don't do anything stupid. But by all means, enjoy yourselves."

Bale and the Women

Baby Boo watched Bale as Jilly and Mole took naps.

In the fire, a log cracked in half, the top end of it upsetting into the ashes below with a thud, and Jilly sat up, brought her rifle to her shoulder, aimed it at Bale. She surveyed the scene. Sat back assured that all was well.

Then Mole sat up, shocked. "What is it?" she yelped.

"Oh ain't you a ninja," Jilly said to her. "Or like a cowboy that sleeps with his eyes open watching the herd for fear of wolves."

"Shut up," said Mole and she laid back on the grass.

"Wait," said Jilly. "Tell him your story."

"Huh?"

"Just the way you told it to me. See if he likes it any better."

"Nah."

"C'mon, Mole, it'll help me get back to sleep."

"Fine." She sat up and faced Bale. "My uncle had a tiny dick," she said. "And it had a funny flavor."

Jilly had a big old grin on, watching Bale to see his reaction. Bale looked at Mole. He looked at Jilly. He looked at Mole again. "Yeah, that's probably all uncles," he told her.

The Stranger

Murk and Mira left the jail and moved in the direction they'd come from, back toward home. They didn't speak. Their tired footsteps caught the street in scuffs and low chatter floated from those who moved along. A passive sense of failure plagued them. Their hearts felt slack and bruised. Low emotions dozed in their stomachs, fluttered like static in their throats.

"All this damn way," Mira said.

"And Bale held hostage."

"I wanna sit down."

They found a makeshift bench in the shade of a ramshackle building that bore a vacancy sign, and they supposed it a kind of inn. "Good a place as any." They moved toward it downheartedly, slunk upon the wooden thing that creaked and shimmied in a way that suggested it might not hold them. Mira cradled her head in her hands, her elbows resting on her knees. Murk thrust his peg leg out toward the dirt road, sat favoring his good leg's ass cheek.

"Could be worse," said Murk.

"How the fuck so?"

A man hoisting a kind of brown stained fabric bundled in a heap came and stood in front of them. He stunk of rotting.

"What is that?" Mira asked. "Take it somewhere else." She held her hand over her mouth and nose like a mask.

"You lost a leg," the man said to Murk.

"Lost ain't quite the right word for it."

"But it's gone, replaced by that peg, and I got an idea. A thing I might part with for the right price."

"You wanna sell us an idea?"

"No, no." He pulled back the fabric to reveal the leg, swollen with rigor mortis.

"What the fuck is that?" Mira said.

"A leg," said the stranger. "Thought you could use it." He motioned the thing toward Murk.

"A rotten leg? For what?"

"For the bones," said the stranger. "Just get rid all this." He took a razor blade from his pocket and began nicking away bits of the gray skin, the darker muscle beneath. Dabs of the leg dropped off to the dirt. "Use the bones instead of the peg."

"No," said Murk. "Get the fuck off out of here and take that foulness with you." Murk stood and pushed the stranger, who dropped the razor, stumbled back a ways then rewrapped the leg.

"This town's just fools," he said. "A perfectly good leg just wasted on all y'all." He kind of held up the leg up for folks to see and walked off toward wherever else he had a mind to go, grumbling nonsense as he went.

"Crazy bastard," said Mira.

Murk shook his hair.

The bits of leg on the road had a funny, yellow shimmer to them. A kind of iridescence to their death.

But then the razor snatched Mira's attention.

"Murk," she said, "what would you do if you couldn't drink shadows?"

Murk's black eyes pondered. "Kill myself," he said.

"That's what I thought," said Mira. "We need to find a mouse."

five

In outer space, unperceived by the naked human eye, traveling at up to forty miles per second, Halley's Comet raced toward its perihelion where it would appear like a blade of white fire slicing across the Earth's aphotic night sky. Its visibility could last weeks, depending on distance and atmospheric conditions. A celestial anomaly that will spook creatures' hearts for certain.

You must understand, for most of collective human consciousness, comets have symbolized God's wrath—black omens of streaking light.

The first known mention of a comet's appearance couples the sighting with an execution. Montezuma saw two comets shortly before Cortes reduced the Aztec civilization to history. This particular comet, Halley's, is credited with William the Conqueror's taking of England, Genghis Khan's invasion of Europe, the birth of Samuel Clemens, and the death of Mark Twain, who claimed "these two unaccountable freaks; they came in together, they must go out together."

Of course, by Twain's time, Halley's Comet was completely accounted for.

Edmond Halley, namesake of the celestial body in question, postulated that perhaps a close-passing comet caused the great flood of

Genesis and Gilgamesh. *Which one motivated that catastrophe is a mystery, but when Halley's Comet passed the Earth in 1682 almost nothing was known about these wonders at all. Halley had, at that time, been studying the strange things for less than two years, and it wouldn't be until 1705 that he would publish his* Synopsis of the Astronomy of Comets, *claiming that recorded sightings in 1531, 1607, and 1682 were all of the same orbiting comet that would come again in 1758.*

In between those two sightings, the one that he saw and the one he predicted, Edmond Halley died. They named the returning comet after him. Since its last pass in 2061, societies have faltered and waned. Anemic versions of civilizations left behind like footprints. Before his death, in what would become the groundwork for actuarial statistics, Edmond Halley proposed that in order for mankind to sustain its population "it is necessary for each married couple to have four children." He came to that conclusion through a deep study of Paris and London, taking into account the typical rate of births, marriages, and deaths in the context of those urban areas' population densities. It's hard to say if he accounted at all for bastard babies, and in the shadow-addicted world, marriages were nearly as rare as comet sightings themselves, but regardless of all that: mankind had not lived up to the numbers, and hardly any humans will see the comet at all.

In outer space, adhering to its orbit, the coma of the comet, a frozen peanut-shaped thing, just a little bigger than Manhattan, races along toward humanity's view.

Murk and the Machine

"Something wrong?" Doc asked.

Murk had taken off his jacket, held it draped over an arm. Black-eyed fools stumbled about the machine, their dark veins throbbing beneath their pale skin, and Murk contemplated them as they staggered. "I wanna try it."

"The machine?" said Doc.

"Yeah. I got this for trade." He lifted up his jacket.

Doc regarded it.

Earlier, Murk and Mira had searched a woodpile for a mouse. It took them nearly an hour of upending logs, but they came on one, and Mira whispered her silent language at it, convinced it to lend assistance. In the pocket of Murk's jacket, it sat hid, the hermit's razor blade accompanying it. The plan was this, the mouse would lay in wait. It would cower in the jacket until taken to the jail, to the cell where Doc kept his things. Once there, the mouse would abscond from the garment, cross into Unlucky Clover's cell, carrying the blade in its mouth, drop the thing close enough so Clover'd notice the implement. In that way, Clover could do the murdering deed for Mira, Murk, and Bale. Off himself and set Mira and her mother free.

"It is a nice jacket," said Doc. "Tell you what. One turn on the machine. One night in the inn. I don't haggle, and I won't entertain haggling."

"Two nights," Murk said. He didn't want to seem too eager.

"One."

The arms and legs dangled. Some of the limbs had already been sipped from. The shadows that remained listed back and forth on the ground.

Mira had made him promise to take the shadow of an arm. "We don't need you any darker than that," she had said, assuming, correctly so, that the smaller quantity of shade produced by an arm would send him into a less-deep stupor, and that if he consumed a leg's worth, Murk would go mad beyond recognition.

"Fine," said Murk. "One night and one swallow."

Doc held out his hand and Murk handed him the jacket. Once the garment traded hands, the shadow of the thing reappeared on the ground. Doc put his face to the jacket, breathed deep its leather scent. "Monroe," he called, and Monroe came running. "Put this in the cell for me and get this man and his friend a room at the inn." And Doc handed the jacket away. "Take your pick," said Doc, and Murk ventured beneath the machine, touched a few of the limbs, stood in the mess of them, the arms and legs dangling down around him like gruesome treasures.

Standing in that wreckage, the smell of near death thick on his tongue, Murk nearly abandoned his notions, nearly dropped to the shadow of a leg, but something at the last minute gave him pause. Perhaps the sound of Mira's voice echoed at him.

He touched a wrist. Ran his fingers toward the elbow. Delicate, but it swayed on its moorings. The hair of it, twinkling in the sun. Murk dropped to the ground. The shadow lay on sand, mysterious now to Murk, strange and delightful.

Murk realized then what it represented. His fake leg tingled, phantom feelings that flittered impossibly. Each of those shadows—or the vacant spaces where shadows should be there on the ground—denoted some horrific amputation, some unwarranted molestation that bore a permanent absence. Murk conceptualized the accosted creatures they belonged to, far away sufferers, most likely with blackened-out eyes. He imagined—in a fascinating moment that seemed unbound by true time—how their lost bodies, those that belonged to these limbs, were elsewhere dawdling through wildernesses or struggling to clutch at some necessary task with a single hand. And then the occasion of the dismemberments occurred to him. In one sharp synapse, some glowing space in his brain, lit up by grievous fantasy, Murk manufactured the dozens of settings that would represent the moments of these limbs being filched off their rightful owners.

In the snag of a river, at the trunk of some live oak, mired in a forgotten town's wreckage, in the crotch of a ravine: the addled personages beset by terrorists, who'd chased down prey in order to offend them forever, placated only by this dastardly deed when shadows were made unavailable to them.

Envision now the victims gulping at shadows with faces terrified, their panic-stricken bodies tangled in shock. Mouths bore open with last-resort binging. Dreadful. Tortuous. Hog-shaped consumption. Savage-streaked gobbling. And the caterwauling of the assailants, robust sermonizing of the pain to come.

Then they produced blades.

Murk's face lost in thought at these dangling limbs.

Murk's mind bereft, crammed down in the cracks of his dark illusioning.

Spent bits of suffering being dealt out like cards.

A counterclockwise circle.

Endlessly moving.

Now at this arm . . .

Now at that leg . . .

Snippets of the slicing, new faces and discomforts.

A bad positioning of blood-slicked limbs. Teeth glimmering absurdly in shrieked-open mouths.

Angry-faced disasters that keep transmitting in Murk's mind.

Hollow and haunting. Shriveled and swollen. Happening the way accidents happen, the way dead children die repeatedly in their mothers' minds daily. For no reason. Set off by some unfair trigger of memory. The shape of an eyebrow. The crack in a sidewalk. The false music of a distant nothing mesmerized by a breeze that isn't even there. And for what? So that we can say of these lost peoples or past tragedies, of these wound scars or cemetery plots that we existed? That we hovered with hearts beating in the motion of the multiverses with minds that could accumulate harms in order to remind us we were alive? That it wasn't all just dreaming. That it can be touched with fingers in the future and that these feelings will launch our hurts anew.

"Son," said Doc, and Murk's face showed shock at him. Doc shook his head, "You don't have all day to choose."

Murk lowered. Sniffed the darkness, felt its odor in his gut like a cramp. His mouth went wet, his skin jittery. He lowered his face. The black magic of his doing it like a dream. The intoxicant was on him even before his lips touched the shade. He huffed and the dim drew from the dirt like a whisper, slithered across his tongue, filled his body with the taste of precious woe, and things got glossy. He could feel his eyes darkening, his skin color draining. His veins thrummed, constricted. Coiled down. Warmed through. A hollow kind of wizardry engulfed him.

The world lurked beneath Murk's understanding.

"What do you think?" said Doc, and the language he manufactured seemed a thing of glass that Murk could rub his fingers over, cut himself with.

He tried to answer, but the ability was lost to him. His mouth felt like a stranger's mouth—like stranger's teeth touched his teeth. Murk stood. The town quivered about him. Had he forgotten how to swallow? Were his hands still his own?

Doc laughed. The laughter squirreled away into the afternoon.

Murk wandered away.

Murk didn't feel like himself.

NEAR DUSK, DOC reached for the pencil behind his ear, set his teeth into it, clicked his tongue. He took the pencil from his mouth, placed it again behind his ear. He paced. He eyed the streets some more. He wiped his palms against his vest. "Monroe," he said, "I imagine the day's done."

Monroe stood from a stool where he had been nearly nodding off. He shook his head to get the blood flowing, his dreadlocks fanning out this way and that. "Want me to throw the switch?"

"Go for it," Doc said. "Close her down." Doc walked off toward the inn, all the townsfolk smiling at him as he passed.

Sunset

"I don't think I'll ever get used to that," Bale said, his eyes on the sunset.

"More small talk?" Jilly asked. She was cleaning her rifle.

"Got any more stories?" Bale asked.

"She doesn't," said Jilly. "She doesn't even really have the one."

Mole threw a pebble at their fire. They'd kept it going the whole day rather than have Baby Boo chance trying to build another. "I got stories," she said.

"Really," said Jilly. "Let's hear one then."

Mole rubbed her chin. "I'm not in the mood."

"Thank fucking God."

"I don't get it," said Bale.

"Well, not everyone's as talkative as you, dome boy. We don't all just love the sound of our own voices and feel compelled to wax philosophical on the sunset and our opinions of it."

"No," said Bale. "What did you guys have to do to get so shafted?"

"Shafted?" said Jilly.

"Seems to me," Bale said, "this is the kind of job you'd get if you were in trouble. Like, back at the train, all the good soldiers were guards and stuff. This child-chasing stuff, following around this redhead and all, seems like a thing you'd do if you pissed someone off or weren't worth much. Like, our equivalent would be latrine detail. Don't get me wrong, that's an admirable job. Hard as fuck though. Like this. Just kind of thankless shit work."

"The good soldiers?" said Jilly. "At the train? What good soldiers might those be? Every time we've gone up against a train we've taken 'em down easy as could be."

"And you've been part of that?"

"Excuse me?"

"You've been there when the trains were taken down? Or were you off chasing a little boy?"

"Mole," said Jilly. "I don't like how he's got me thinking."

"Everyone in our army has an important job," Mole said to Bale. "We've been at trains before. Right now, we're here."

"Sure," said Bale. "But that doesn't mean that some jobs aren't more important than others. Chasing a little boy is very important, but it's probably not as important as attacking a train. Right?"

"Can we shoot him right now?" said Jilly.

"No."

"Why not then?"

"Because we promised."

"So, in your army," continued Bale. "What would you have to do to get a more important, important job?"

"Yeah?" Jilly asked Mole. "What would we have to do?"

Mole messed with a fingernail. "I guess we'd have to prove ourselves, somehow."

"Seems to me," said Bale, "y'all should get on figuring out how to do that. Instead of sitting around bickering about who tells the shittiest stories, or whatever." Bale looked away from them. "But that's just, like, small talk."

The fire crackled. The sun set.

Doc and Mira

Doc saw Mira sitting on a rickety bench, her head hung, elbows on her knees.

"Got problems?"

Mira shook her head. "I'm fine."

"You have a room," Doc said. "Your friend and I traded." Doc stood then in front of Mira, his eyes filled with gladness. "Come in, we'll get you set up."

"I stuck my head in there earlier. Looks a little rough."

"It is, but I told you earlier. Won't nobody bother you. I know what it's like to travel far for no reason. You drink?"

"Drink?"

"Moonshine."

"I've had fruit wine before. It made me feel funny."

"It's supposed to. C'mon."

They entered the inn and the place went quiet. Every eye in the saloon aimed at Doc. A one-armed man raised his good hand which clutched a glass. His hook-shaped nose seemed daffy. "To Doc," he hollered, and the whole bar toasted. "To Doc," they said in unison, his name coming out slurred and grand. The one-armed man set his glass down, ran his fingers through his stringy hair.

Doc shooed off the gesture, and the crowd got noisy.

"You're famous," said Mira.

Doc shrugged. "They don't want to end up like Clover."

They approached the bar, and the bartender skipped the other drinkers, handed Doc two glasses and a bottle of moonshine. "Over here," said Doc, and the two moved to a yellow-pine bench on the far wall from the piano. The music chimed in whacky fashion. The chatter of the fellow drinkers clucked out like white noise. They sat down and Doc uncorked the bottle. He poured for Mira first, then himself. "It's strong."

Mira sniffed the spirit. It smelled like fire. She put the glass to her lips, let it roll to her tongue. The tiniest swallow. "Whoo," she said, lowering the glass. "What's it made from?" She licked her lips madly, breathed with a wide opened mouth.

Doc drained his glass, poured another. "Stuff."

Mira raised her glass to her lips. The second sip was easier.

Doc said, "Tell me about you."

"Nothing to tell." Her eyes so gentle.

"Sure there is. We all got stories or lies. Live near?"

"Not too far off. With my mom."

"She still have her shadow?"

"Had it stolen."

"My mother was the same, and I do not miss that taste."

"Taste?"

"They're all the same," said Doc. "Mine liked rabbit shadows."

"Mine likes birds."

"Hell that's not so bad. At least they're in the right direction. Up in the sky, their shadows falling on the ground. The ground critters—squirrels, rabbits, possums, rats—you have to catch them. I thought of the machine on account of her. It turned out different than I figured. She was dead by the time I had it built. She probably wouldn't have liked it anyhow. These people," he pointed to the folks about, "human shade is what they're all about."

"You get sick of being around them? All the unruliness." Men were shoving men. At the pool table, a woman with black eyes lined up a shot.

"Not really. Sometimes I miss arguments. Most everyone here just agrees with me." Doc poured Mira more moonshine. He motioned across to the bartender to come around, and he trotted over, smelling like bleach. "Monroe told you about a room earlier?"

"Yes, sir."

"It belongs to her," Doc pointed to Mira.

"Sure thing," the bartender said. He fished a key from his pocket and handed it to her.

Doc filled and drained his glass again. He passed the bottle and the glass to the bartender. "Well," Doc said. "I'll now retire."

"Wait," Mira said, "there's no way to fix what they got? Your mom? Mine?"

Doc looked at his feet. "It is a thing I puzzle over still. If my mom was alive, I could take her apart. I could hang each of her arms from my machine. Each of her legs. Those I could get the shadow back for. But even if I did, if I took them off the machine, put them back on her body, even if the shock of all that cutting and reattaching didn't kill her, the way surgery can, I don't think her shadow would come back. It's something in the mind or soul. Used to, they called it turning the sun to darkness. But I don't know if that's how it works. My father thought if we just thought about shadows the right way, the riddle of it would become clear to us. I've thought about them every way I could."

Mira sipped her moonshine again.

"You don't have to pretend you like it."

"I'm coming around to it, I think."

"People do," said Doc.

Mira was moonshine loose, fuddled. The noise of the inn happened around them.

Doc waved goodbye.

Mira nursed her glass and watched the insanity unfold.

Murk so Dark

It was night when Murk showed up at the inn. He had a lost expression on his face, a sort of spooked, empty grin. Mira was half loopy. Her hair hung across her eyes. She waved at him. "Murk," she hollered. She stood, grabbed his arm, dragged him to a seat near the pool table. "This guy can't play piano for shit." Broken notes fluttered about. "Where've you been?"

"I can't really hear."

Mira hollered, "Where've you been?"

Murk pointed to the door he just came through.

"You're like, so fucked up," Mira said. Her head muddy with moonshine, her eyes sort of trundling, but she could make out his super darkness. "You okay?"

Murk's black eyes like giant nothings in his head, moved over Mira entirely. From her toes to her eyes. He licked at his lips. The music bounced and jangled. The smell of strangers getting sloppy. "Maybe."

The music stopped and the one-eyed midget came waddling

over from the pianola. "Any requests?" he asked, his voice quasi-maniacal.

"I can barely remember my name," Murk said.

"Wait," said Mira, "ooh," she kind of clapped her hands, "know any Doors?"

"Do *I* know any Doors?" said the midget. "That's my fucking band. I know 'Light my Fire' and I know 'Love Me Two Times.'"

"Play 'em both," said Mira.

"Fuckin A," said the midget, and he went back to the pianola and started banging away, lowing the lyrics.

"You know that it would be untrue . . ."

Mira and Murk listened a bit. Murk kind of chewing nothing, drumming the fingers of one hand on a knee. Mira bobbed her head. Murk cleared his throat. "This sucks," said Murk.

"I told you, he can't play for shit."

Murk clicked his tongue. "It's not that. The whole thing sucks. The words. The music. Every single part of it sucks."

Murk reached down for Mira's empty glass. "I'll be right back," he said, and Mira listened to the music as Murk went up to the bar. She looked around at everyone. Tried to guess at what they were. Like, beyond people. How did they get along? What did they do to occupy their time? That seemed the strangest task of a life—all the slow moments between the good and bad things. But then she thought, *What was she?* Mira—finder of wild shade, scrambler of eggs. Murk was a shadow addict. Bale a domer, or ex-domer. A dishwasher. A pointer of guns. Haver of a Mohawk, now. *Mira*, she thought, *cutter of hair*. And around this time Murk showed up with two full glasses and a pair of scissors. "You're a fucking mind reader, Murk!"

"What?"

Mira reached for the glass, the scissors.

Murk handed her the glass but kept the scissors. "I can do it," he said.

"I owe you," said Mira.

"Owe me something else." Murk began to blindly cut locks from his head, and they dropped on his lap and on the floor around him, but everyone who noticed his doing the task seemed to treat it like some normal, anytime thing.

Mira drank and Murk hacked his hair, and the midget started the second song and Mira asked, "Like this one better?"

"Fuh-uh," said Murk. "And now you can't say I got your hair anymore." He took a few more hacks at it before leaning back into his seat, sipping at his moonshine.

"Nope," said Mira, "now you got butchered-ass hair. Like that Unlucky Clover."

"Shit," said Murk, "start that and I'll make you my creature."

"Gross."

"We got a room," said Murk. "You could be my creature." He weirded up his face. "Creature," he said. "Creature."

"Fuck that," said Mira, and then they were both kind of laughing.

But some darkness fluttered in Murk. A quandary developed. Some equation he would've normally terminated travelled toward a bad solution. "Why haven't we ever though?" Murk asked. "I've known you a long time."

Mira considered it. "*Creatured?*"

"No," said Murk. "But, like, normal."

"Dunno. Just never been like that."

246 BRIAN ALLEN CARR

"Let's make it like that then." He had a garbage expression in his eyes. "We could go to the room and fuck."

"What? No way. You're not being you."

"C'mon."

"Let's talk about something else. I'm serious." Her eyes found the pool table. "If Bale was here, you guys could play pool. I bet you'd beat him."

Murk puffed up a bit. Shadow stretching his eyes. "Do you fuck Bale?" he asked. "Is that what the deal is?"

"Oh, my God, Murk. What the fuck? Be you."

"This is me," he said, "this is how much shadow I should always have." His words seemed to come from another dimension, and the noise gained the attention of the room.

The pianola player ceased to play. From behind the bar, the bartender emerged. He came to them, propped his hip against the pool table, picked up a cue. "He bothering you ma'am?"

"The fuck do you care?" asked Murk.

The bartender seemed tired. "Normally, sir, I wouldn't, but I've got orders to make sure she's not disturbed. Might I suggest . . ."

"I don't take suggestions."

"What about orders?" the bartender said. The customers of the place seemed to amass behind him in support. "Because we can make it an order, if we need to."

Murk grunted, gandered at the crowd. "Fuck it." His head bloomed then a bit. Swelled up with anger. Thinned out and enlarged.

"Do you take suggestions?" the bartender asked Mira. "You could retire to your room. Top of the stairs, second door on your left."

Mira made to go, to retreat from Murk's grossness. "Will you be okay?"

"Fuck do you care?"

She stood, passed through the peculiar crowd, climbed the stairs. She looked back down. All the black eyes peered at her with madness. All the pale faces and dicey figures. The dusty room, a sort of forgotten and bad feeling to it.

Murk yelled up at her. "Bet you wish you'd left me in that fucking tree, huh?"

Mira didn't know what to think.

She turned and made her way into the room.

It was lit with a ghostly electric light. Blue shadows seemed to hover on all things. The bed sagged in the middle, felt soft, revolted her. The blankets were pilly and the pillows hard. She stared at the ceiling, a sort of grisly nervousness on her skin.

BELOW, MURK GUZZLED moonshine and half-danced to the bad music and draped his arms over strangers' shoulders and spun with them across the floor. They were toasting and whooping and careening and making merry, and a lady with bad teeth pressed her face to his face, the lids of her eyes painted purple with makeup. They became inseparable in the revelry, fastened to each other with some lust-fashioned adhesive. She didn't strike his fancy in any way beyond his body being desirous, and they kissed often with heaved-open mouths, kneading their tongues into one another's tongues, a sort of mucking of orifices.

If she had a name, Murk never learned it. And the crowd about them blurred into noise and dropped free of them and they were ascending the stairs.

They dribbled into disarray. The yelping of their carnalities dictating endeavors.

Inside a room, filled with raucous caterwauling from the saloon below, Murk explored the flubbed body of his partner, her blemished skin and skeletal protrusions, the reek of neglect, sour stench of vicious years.

Tussling into the corruption of it, Murk grabbed at her skull, lifted away a mottled hairpiece he hadn't recognized was false, and the blonde wiglet flopped in his fist as she tore open his shirt and licked her way down his belly, and his black eyes were at the ceiling then, and his ears filled with explosions.

Bits were lost.

Now he is on top of her, the mattress swaying.

Standing then, she on the bed.

Bent over.

Spread somewhat.

Night shattering like cymbals. Percussion and cacophony.

All this time, in these actions, a sort of to and fro.

Intermittently, making eye contact. Anger maybe? A pinch of violence?

Who was she even?

For that matter, who was he?

The fake blonde hair clutched in his fist like a hammer.

Sometimes bad decisions keep lasting forever.

Razor Blade

Joe Clover came conscious in the night. He tossed quickly, batted his face with his palms. Had something been on him? His head ached. His body felt poisonous.

He sat up, his legs crossed. His eyes seemed lost in the dark, but incrementally shapes became clear. The toilet, for instance. Its metallic bowl glinting what light there was. The odor of urine was permanent but seemed advanced now, so Clover stood up and flushed, sat back on the ground as the thing filled with fresh water.

It was then he saw the mouse. It came scampering across the floor, and his eyes followed the path of it. An entertainment of sorts. He'd gotten used to them. Roaches too. Before, he'd see a bug and get squeamish, fill with anger and hew the thing down with his heel. But now, so long lonely in his state of capture, he welcomed any creature that might chance to share his cell.

It bounded along but paused at some object. It ran a circle around the thing. Clover couldn't tell what it was. He neared it, and the mouse tarried off. Clover stopped. Slowed. He wanted the mouse to stay. In all honesty, he wished to touch it. Gently. Perhaps the back of his finger across the top of its head, and, if he was lucky, maybe the little mouse would lean into his touch, stay on there in that place with him to offer some kind of company.

But, it was not to be. The closer he got, the further the mouse moved. However, the thing. That it had run a circle round. On the floor like a jewel. It glistened.

Clover didn't believe it. A razor? He fist-rubbed his eyes.

He pressed the pad of his thumb against it firmly and it stuck to his skin, and he lifted his hand and the thing just stayed pressed there. He turned it in the light. A twinkle ran down the blade, dimmed where the thing was nicked. He gripped, raked the implement across the thumbnail of his other hand and flecks of the nail shaved toward the ground.

Joy filled him.

He looked toward the sky.

"Thank you," he said to whatever.

Then, taking the blade, he ran the sharp edge up his arm, passing it through the thick veins of his wrist, and bands of blood slipped down toward his fingers, dripped in beads to the dirty ground. He traded the blade to his now weakened grip, the sticky blood flooding across the thing as he made at the other arm, hacking less precisely, but still rendering damage, he let open his other wrist, gushing indignation. His life spilling out of him. His freedom on its way.

Doc Rages

He woke early as with all days and called for his mug of coffee to drink as he dressed. Servants attended him always. They stood in wait, watched over his possessions, guarded his holdings in the night. Coffee, for instance, was a luxury most couldn't afford. Indeed, even the brew Doc got was a thin strain of the stuff. More hot water than anything else, maybe the smell of beans coming across in the steam, but only faintly. His stores of it were under lock and key. Ancient cans reclaimed from refuse piles and abandonments, brought to him by patrons who knew Doc was a man of fine tastes.

Once ready, he stepped into the streets, still except for his motions and the doings of a few folks under his employ. He prided himself on being an early riser, liked to take to the dawn-lit streets with gusto.

He moved briskly toward his machine, the morning almost glowing, and he tossed back the canvas covers to inspect aspects of the device. Chiefly, he was concerned with append-ages. He studied them for signs of struggle, decay. If they seemed chafed or ashy, he wiped them with lotion. If their bandages had gone soggy, he'd wind away the spent gauze and replace that with fresh. He hummed softly as he did this, a dignity in his laboring.

Once certain that all things were in order, Doc would take to a stool, cross his arms and sit satisfied.

But this morning an off stillness plagued him.

He had some disquieting premonition, and around this time he heard his name called.

"Doc," his name came again.

It was Monroe and he was agitated, running toward Doc from the doorway of the jail.

"Doc, Doc," he hollered again. "You gotta come see."

Doc was rarely yelled for, so he knew a notable thing had occurred. He pitched what was left of his coffee and stood, made his way to Monroe who had paused in his proceeding and was now merely waving at Doc to come.

He and Monroe entered the jail.

On the ground, Joe Clover lay dead—the odd smell of new death and the queer stillness of a freshly departed soul haunted the jail.

"What the hell happened?" Doc asked, but Monroe said nothing. "Wasn't a guard on duty?"

"All night."

"Who the fuck? Which-a one?"

"Bones."

Doc yanked the keys from the wall and snatched open the cell, the cage door clanging against the concrete wall. He jumped inside and dropped to his knees near the body. "Call Bones," said

Doc, and he clenched his jaw and his fists and waited sternly for his failed guardsman.

Bones held his hat when he showed, twitching like a kicked dog.

Doc barked up at him. "Care to explain?"

Bones's eyes filled with awe. "I have no idea."

"You watched the door?"

"All night."

"No coming or going?"

"Not at all."

Doc found the razor sunk in Clover's spilled blood, and fished it out, held it in his fingers. "How'd he get this?"

"I haven't the foggiest," said Bones.

Doc wiped blood on his pants. "That girl," he said. "Her friend."

"Maybe tossed it to him? When y'all came in?" Monroe said.

"Couldn't have," said Doc. "I'd've seen it done. Shit," he said. He pocketed the blade and stepped to the sink and cleaned his hands proper. "But let's fucking find 'em."

The three moved from the jail and prowled toward the inn. There seemed a rage in all their eyes. The purpose which drove them was palpable.

Into the inn they strode, a general and his conscripts. Doc took a look at the fatigue and disarray set in on the establishment, "Would it kill you to clean a bit?" he screamed.

The bartender stood from behind the bar, a green hue to his face. A thick sickness in his visage. "Sorry, Doc," he said.

"The girl?"

"What?" said the bartender. He grabbed a pitcher and brought it toward his face like he might vomit.

"Oh hell. From last night. The stranger girl." Doc started up the stairs, pointed toward the rooms. "Which one?"

The bartender held up a finger.

"One?"

He shook his head. "No," he said and gagged. "Three." Then he coughed up some yuck, caught it in the receptacle.

Doc wasted no time. He stormed to three and kicked in the door, and it burst wide, splinters coughing off the jamb, and Mira shot up wide eyed from her bed, clutching blankets to her chest.

"How'd you do it?" Doc asked her.

Mira rubbed her eyes. "I won't tell you anything."

Murk in Disgust

His eyes fired open and his heart filled with haunts.

What had he done?

Vague threads of the night before came back to him and he gazed about feverishly. The thing, as it was that he now considered her, with which he'd spent the night, lay passed out, her face smothered into a pillow, so only her skull showed to his eyes, with its patchy, thin hair clinging to it like spiderwebs. She seemed skeletal in her repose. A crypt thing out of its resting place. There were crude tattoos across the wrinkly skin of her back. Varicose veins rose from her legs, everywhere.

From beyond his door, Murk heard commotion. Tussling and hollering and then heavy steps on the stairs.

He fumbled from the mattress and crept to the window to watch the street below.

Doc and Monroe dragged Mira toward the jail, Mira screaming at some point, "I ain't telling nothing."

They handled her roughly.

Murk set to thought.

Of all the bad doings for which his behavior brought to fruition, this was the worst of it. It had been intended, as planned before Murk visited the machine, that they'd meet up as soon as able and leave town together. His conversation. The haircutting. It came back to him in lewd heaves, and he curled up with his hands holding his head, disgusted at himself for how he'd behaved. But could he fix it? His head spun circles, but he seemed clearer minded than the night prior.

Murk scrutinized the nude thing on the bed.

Was this why the leaving hadn't happened?

Murk went to the door and put his ear to it. He could hear conversation below, so he cracked the door and stared down into the saloon.

"Think," some stranger was hollering at the bartender, who was doubled over with his face in a pitcher's mouth. "Where'd he go?"

The bartender shook his head and puked some, and Murk eased the door closed.

He probed the room, surveying the situation.

When he saw the wig, his escape plan came clear to him.

Mira the Prisoner

She'd been deposited in the cell with Clover and the door had been locked tight. She pressed against the wall, slumped to the ground, mortified.

"How?"

"I don't know anything," said Mira.

"Earlier," said Doc, "you said you wouldn't *tell* anything."

"What's the difference?"

"At this moment," Doc said, "I don't know. I'm not sure what I think should happen to you on account. But I am certain of this. You're gonna stay in there until I figure it out. And he's gonna stay in there with you." He motioned to dead Joe Clover. "And I am a patient man. If it takes me a year to decide your fate, so be it."

Doc left the jail.

Mira hid her eyes from her dead cellmate.

Murk the Woman

He looked in the mirror and messed with the wig some more—blonde and a bit tiny on his noggin, stringy and napped. The dress's neckline was low, showed off the hairs on his chest, was tight on his shoulders. He couldn't fit his foot in her shoe, so he kept his boot on.

"Heinous," Murk said to his reflection, but then he saw the dress's owner in her stew, and decided that the black garment probably looked better on him by a bit.

He closed his eyes at his reflection, opened them, said, "Let's see how it goes."

Murk opened the door and made his way to the staircase. When he got to the top of it, the bartender hollered. "You see that stranger last night?"

"I did not," said Murk. He made no attempts to disguise his voice. He figured, if his chest didn't give him away, nothing would.

The bartender nodded up at him, puked a bit more, and Murk climbed down the stairs, his peg tapping as he descended.

He crossed the saloon. Regal, sort of, in his getup.

He stepped out into the street. All the light of the world.

No one seemed to be watching him. He turned left. He headed out of town. He sort of had a plan.

JILLY SAW HIM first. She had her eyes to a pair of binoculars and was surveying the distance for Murk and Mira. "Well," she said to Bale. "I thought maybe this was them, but it appears to be some kind of hideous, one-legged woman. So I might get to shoot you still."

"Lucky me," said Bale.

"Wait, wait," said Jilly. "She's taken her hair off and looks even worse."

Mole was juggling a few rocks she'd found. "Taken it off?"

"Like a wig maybe," said Jilly. "Oh, hang on. Maybe." Jilly lowered the binoculars and went to Bale. His hands were still tied behind his back. "Look that way," Jilly said. "That your friend?"

It took Bale a second. "Focus," he said. Jilly turned the focus wheel. "Stop. What the hell?"

"Is it him?" Mole asked.

"Yeah, but where's Mira?"

Murk started waving his wig toward them all. "Don't shoot," he hollered out, his voice thinly coming from the distance.

"You can ask him when he gets here," said Jilly, and, when he finally walked up, she said, "You make an ugly bitch."

"Thanks," said Murk. "I need some water."

Mole handed him a canteen.

"Where the fuck's Mira?" Bale asked.

Murk motioned back toward the town. He swallowed hard, cleared his throat. Every eye in the small encampment was locked on him. "I got good news and bad news."

"The fuck you mean bad news?" said Bale.

"And good." Murk took another sip.

It was quiet.

"Well, let us have it," said Jilly. "No need to gather further invitation."

"The good news is," Murk said, "I found your friend."

"Friend?" said Mole.

Murk held his hand up to his chest, palm toward the earth. "Round this high tall. Redheaded. Tells people to suck on his dick and such. Paints skulls on stuff."

Jilly clapped her hands. "That's our shithead for certain," she said.

"But," said Murk, "it's complicated."

"Complicated?" Mole dropped her rocks.

"Mira and I were hoping to do y'all a solid. We thought we'd planned it out perfect."

"Planned what?" said Bale.

Murk stared at Bale hard, trying to convey something. "A jailbreak. They got him in a cell back there. Guarded." He sipped again from the canteen.

"Well shit," said Jilly, "he probably deserves it." She looked at Mole. "What do ya think? That good enough just knowing that? Take the news to his mom."

"But what about Mira?" Bale asked. He kicked dirt at Murk.

"That's the bad news. We were trying to get him out of there. We were worried about you. We thought if we came back and just said we'd seen him that it wouldn't be enough. We figured we'd get him out and, like, use him as trade. We'd come to camp with him as a hostage, a knife to his neck or something, and say that we wouldn't give him up unless they gave you up, but Mira got caught in our trying, and right now, they got 'em both in the same cell.

Sitting in the center of town. And I don't know what they've got planned for them, but my guess is a hanging. They got some kind of scaffolding built, it looks like. Not far from the jail."

"That settles it then," Jilly said. "We wait for him to hang, and we go in to round up his corpse. Take him back to the Founder, let her know we tried."

"It does not settle a damn thing," said Mole. "Shit. Listen to you. I'd rather him just disappear than our showing up with his neck-broken body. You ever see a hanged man? Their heads go a willy-nilly, and often their eyes pop from their skulls. We'd get demoted, showing up with him like that."

"Then what, Mole? Go in there guns blazing?"

"Normally, I wouldn't suggest it, but look at these past few days. This past outing. I'm done chasing this boy, and maybe the domer is right. Our going in there might be a way to get a more important, important job. Worst case, we get killed and don't have to worry about any of it anymore anyway."

Jilly looked so proud. "You're the boss," she said. She grinned at Baby Boo, "Ash your eyes, bitch! We're gonna murder some black-blooded scoundrels."

The three women went then to the fire, and Mole grabbed some dark soot and distributed it as they made ready, clucking incantations at one another as they rimmed their eyes with black.

Bale whispered to Murk. "The redhead? I thought you . . ."

"I did."

"So what the fuck?"

"The other part's true. The Mira part. They got her, man. And I ain't got no better ideas."

Bale nodded. He didn't either.

Doc Shuts Down
the Machine

It was only late afternoon, but Doc motioned for Monroe to flip the switch early.

"You okay, Doc, you don't seem yourself?"

"Monroe, I am bothered. That is the only word for it. I've been thinking about it all day. What is it? I keep asking myself. Doc, I say, what is it that you feel? Earlier I toyed with the term depressed. But I think depression implies a sort of sedentary reaction, a sort of letting the world happen and feeling small against the happening of it. Then I tried molested, but that word is too sexual in nature, and it also implies that something was done to me, and that's not really the case. Something was done to a possession of mine. I do not feel swindled, because that girl told me her intentions, and I don't feel naïve, because I knew that if given the opportunity to disobey me she would have taken it. I suppose I overestimated myself. So, it might be that I feel susceptible, but all that really means is I feel affected. So, I ask myself then, what is the nature of this affectation? And so, bothered is what I've come to decide is how I feel. Sort of troubled by the pestering of others. It seems like a generalization that, but I assure you I've come to it after much deliberation."

"But you still want me to throw the switch, right?"

"Yes, Monroe, I do," said Doc, and he sat on his bench and watched for the day to gray.

Plan of Attack

Once the women had ashed their eyes and had loaded up their rifles and had chanted their war cries, the five made ready to head toward town.

"Y'all are just staying back," Jilly said to Murk and Bale. "You'll just get in the way."

"What's the plan?" asked Murk.

"You don't need to know," said Mole.

"You're at least waiting till sundown, right?"

"Sunset," said Mole. "We'll enter the town from the west and the sun will be behind us and it'll disorient them and we'll have good light by which to aim our rifles."

"Yeah," said Murk, "but your shadows will be as long as they can get."

"What?"

"They'll drink them," said Murk. "That's the first thing they'll try to do."

"You see my shadow on the ground?"

"Forgot," Murk said.

"I'm a pretty good shot," said Bale. "If you want to untie me and give me a rifle."

"Truth is," said Jilly, "I'm not really sure of your status. You might should be shot dead right now, and you're probably most definitely a prisoner of war."

"But Murk came back."

"But our promise was to the girl," said Jilly. "Not this black-eyed she-man."

Murk tugged at his dress. "I'm kind of getting used to it," he said. "Lets the breeze in." He walked over near the fire and picked up the Dutch oven. It had been taken out of the ashes and had cooled enough to carry.

"What the hell you doing with that?" Jilly asked.

"It's Mira's," he said. "I'm taking it back to her."

Doc in Thought

But maybe depressed *was* the right word. The sun was setting and Doc sat on his bench, thinking about it. He fetched lines of poetry from his mind, whispered them as he watched the day go:

> *Till when they reached the other side,*
> *A dominie in gray*
> *Put gently up the evening bars,*
> *And led the flock away.*

Was he bereaved? Did Clover's passing do that to him? He always hated the man, but now that he was dead, did his absence create some kind of void in him?

Monroe walked up with a bottle of spirits and a glass and handed the two things to Doc, but Doc declined the glass, instead dislodging the cork and sipping straight from the bottle.

"Anything else I can bring you, sir?"

"I don't think so." And, in all that, he never took his eyes off the sun.

"I'll be at the inn saloon a bit, and I'll stick my head out every so often to check."

"Mighty kind of you, Monroe, but I imagine I'll be fine. Enjoy yourself, I guess. Do whatever you feel."

Monroe shrugged, made off silently, going back to the deformed music and festivities at the saloon.

Smote maybe? But that just suggested a general striking of feeling. Pangs. But what is a pang anyhow? The shape of the feeling more than the feeling itself, as it occurred to Doc. How the feeling came at you. In a pang. But this feeling was like a long thick thing. An oppression? A setting down upon? As though burdened by a bother. A bother of someone else's forming and for someone else's pleasure.

Saddled?

Shit. He felt saddled.

That's what it was.

Not only by the girl who'd done in Clover, but by all of it. The town. The shadow addicts.

Look how much he had done. Look how much order he had given his little corner of the world.

And for what? What was the trade? What had he asked in turn?

That he be allowed his prisoner. That if he felt so inclined to keep a man in a cage in misery for eternity, he be given that privilege.

But now that Clover was dead, the ungrateful repayment for all his labors seemed to stick the saddle firmly on him. He felt a beast of burden. "Sure, Doc will carry the weight of you all," he thought. "Sure, Doc will hold the load."

He drank more. He beheld the thinning sun.

He half thought about tearing the whole place down.

Tearing the
Whole Place Down

But Doc would have to get in line.

They came with violence in their hearts and discipline in their steps.

Jilly came from the north. Mole from the east and Baby Boo from the west.

The idea was not to get in and out unnoticed.

"We'll leave no one alive, save a few to spread the word of us. The Founder needs to know what we're capable of."

Mole's orders, and so be it.

Carnage was the course of action.

The women soldiers affixed bayonets to their rifles, walked stealth-like with their barrels raised. Just because they wanted to take the fight to them, didn't mean they wouldn't use the element of surprise.

"Don't shoot till you see the whites of their eyes," Jilly joked, and she tiptoed down the road, staying near the buildings, headed for the hum of the inn.

Once there, hid up in shadow, the glow of the electric lights pulsing out in the dusk-laden street, Jilly lit a coal-oil explosive and lobbed it at the bat-wing doors of the place, and it burst open into flames which spat beyond the entrance, and the merriment making inside transformed to commotion and folks spilled toward the street.

That's when the rifles rang out. Some ten or twelve of the saloon patrons were mowed down before they realized the trap. Most likely, they thought some mere fire had broken out, but when folks started falling out with holes in their heads, pushed back into the saloon by projectiles after trying to flee outdoors for safety, the realization of an aggression became clear to them.

"Quit playing the fucking piano," someone screamed, but the thing still twinkled on in absurd fashion.

Murk and Bale were a bit down the road, watching it all go down. Thick heaves of smoke stenched up the air.

"You think you can untie my wrists?" Bale asked.

Murk raised the Dutch oven he held. "My hands are full."

"How many people you think they've killed so far?"

"Sixteen?"

From the second story window of the inn, a bald, naked woman dove into the street, landing on her feet, running toward the women soldiers, a razor blade in each hand, slicing in every direction at once, or at least trying to. Jilly ran her bayonet through her throat, kicked her to the ground.

"Seventeen?"

However many folks there were in the town, it seemed almost painfully clear that aside from those in the inn, there'd be few to lend assistance. If folks were in the surrounding buildings, they were staying hid up in them.

The women moved into the inn methodically, shooting and knifing all those who had the misfortune of being there.

Only a few of the men gave fight.

They had crude weaponry, shovel handles and table legs, which they swung frantically, but the women had been trained to fight soldiers, and made quick work of them. Jilly was especially pleased at herself when she took a machete from a one-armed weirdo with a hooknose and used the thing to hack off his other arm. The blade was dull, so it took some doing, but it was worth it to her.

The man scowled down at the spot she fought the arm off from. "Bitch, bitch, bitch" he kept calling. Then Jilly hit him in the head with his own arm, dropped the thing and fired a shot between his eyes and a belch of his brain popped out the back of his head, spritzed the liquor bottles behind the bar with gray matter.

For a few minutes, the melee was obscene. The screaming and gunfire and the begging and pleading. The smell of blood and gunpowder. Fire and spilled booze.

"Don't kill me, don't . . ." but they were already dead.

After a bit, it quieted down, only the crackling of the inn on fire providing a kind of background score to the quick defeat, and then the piano caught ablaze and its strings popped and hollered making some murderous music.

Broken bottles rolled about, tinkling. Moonshine dripped from surfaces like rain.

Jilly stepped from the inn, her face soot smeared, holding her newly acquired machete.

And that's when Murk and Bale saw it.

Above Jilly in the deep-dark distance.

Like a miniature fist of light throwing a haymaker across the heavens, Halley's Comet hung.

Jilly appeared glorious beneath it.

Some countess of the apocalypse come to carry off souls in a cauldron.

"Where's this goddamned jail?" she screamed.

Murk tilted his head in the direction and Jilly stomped off proudly, unaware.

"Is that it?" said Bale, his eyes glued to the comet.

"Gotta be," said Murk. The streaking thing of white against the navy, sullen sky.

"And Clover?" Bale asked. "Y'all get him?"

Then they heard the bang.

Jilly and Murk

When Mole entered the jail, the damage was done.

"What happened?" she said to Jilly, who laid on the ground bleeding.

"That motherfucker shot me." Doc lay dead on the ground, a machete blade through his face. In his hands, he cradled some ancient musket. A single-shot kind of thing with a six-foot barrel.

Mole lowered herself to Jilly to inspect her. Baby Boo came running in, followed by Murk and Bale. Mira screamed with joy when she saw the boys.

"Will I make it?" Jilly asked.

"I don't think so," said Mole

"That fucking sucks." Her eyes went every which way. Came back to Mole's eyes.

"I'm sorry."

"It hurts like a thing there's no cuss big enough for." She looked down at her stomach. You could've fit a child's fists in the wound. "I can't make it stop bleeding."

"Don't try. Just let it go."

"Easy for you to say."

Mole touched Jilly's brow. "Wanna hear a story?"

"You fucking serious?" Jilly's face spasmed with pain. "You fucking with me now?"

"It's good. I just thought of it."

Jilly rolled her eyes. Swallowed hard. Her face was sweaty and pale. "Ain't like I could stop you."

"I once had a friend named Jilly," Mole said. "And my stories bored her to death."

Jilly giggled some. "You're making me bleed more," she said. Her eyes went wide at nothing and she was gone.

Mole gaped over at the cell. "Where's the redhead?"

She eyed Murk. Murk tilted the Dutch oven as if offering it away.

Then, "I knew'd you was lying," Baby Boo screamed. A rifle went off and the Dutch oven clanged to the ground. Murk heaped back at the wall behind him, dragged to the floor. Black blood smearing the wall as he dropped off with closed eyes.

Mole jumped up, stepped toward Baby Boo. "Your year starts again," she said, and Baby Boo broke down into sobbing and Mole ordered her out of the jail.

But Mira was crying too, and the jail was thick with panic. Great sobs and confusion.

"You," Mole said to Bale. "Come with me." She grabbed him by his ear and tugged him along. She took the cell keys from a hook on the wall and unlocked the door, forced Bale into the quarters along with Mira and dead Clover. Locked the door of the thing. Pitched the keys at Murk's bloody guts.

"I never want to see either of you ever again." She hoisted Jilly over her shoulder and walked her into the night. For a solid hour Bale and Mira listened to Mole and Baby Boo working their way through the town, killing whoever was left.

Then, the craziest thing, Murk's eyes opened wide. He looked about. "They gone?" he asked.

Mira jumped up, grabbed the cell bars, leaned into them hard as though she might be able to push through them. "Murk," she sobbed. "You okay?"

"Oh, fuck no." He said. "I don't know what all the bullet got, but most nothing on me's working. Look at my right hand."

Mira did, and he was wagging his middle finger back and forth.

"It's the only movement I got left, and I'm gonna keep doing it till I can't no more."

"That's fine," Mira said.

"You sure," said Bale. He had dragged up to the bars. The shaved part of his head cool against the iron. "Can't just toss the keys at us?"

"Keys?"

"On your stomach," said Mira.

"Yup," said Murk. "Can't do shit about it."

"It's okay," said Bale. "Just relax."

Murk looked down at his hand. "It stopped," he said.

"Short lived," said Mira.

Murk laughed. "Shit," he said, "she's right. The laughing and bleeding. They're tied together somehow."

"Murk," said Mira, "do you remember any of it?"

Murk lowered his eyes. A million moments rolled into a breath. "All of it," he said.

"Not me," said Mira. "Last thing I remember is we were walking to town. And then somehow you got me my pot back. In between, I've forgotten."

Murk smiled black blood at her. "I was thinking," he said, "when you get back," he coughed some and redness bloomed at the corner of his lips, "if it didn't work. Our killing Clover. Just tell your mom to change her mind. Tell her that it's fair now." His eyes dropped to his shot-open belly. "That this makes it fair. You know?"

"Okay," said Mira.

"Cause you owe me," Murk said. "On account of my jacket."

Mira motioned to the other cell. "I'll be able to get it back for you soon," she said, "your jacket."

"Nope," said Murk. "It'd never be the same."

Then he quit breathing and his eyes got gray and Mira had never before seen them that color, and she wasn't certain if that's the true color they were, or if they'd been stained that way somehow by Murk's lifestyle.

envoi

Father and Son

Across that world, the inhabitants were caught in personal adventures. Mira, Murk, and Bale had their thing, but elsewhere similar missions were underway. Dome people boarded trains; warring women loaded rifles. Symbiotic, perhaps.

Not too far away, a lesser but similar journey was afoot. A man named Jessup helped his father Rondell along toward a hopeful murder that could never occur. They'd been traveling for days and days across inhospitable terrain, entirely ill-equipped for their expedition. This is the thing about people: they overestimate themselves or underestimate the world. They see mountains on the horizon and they set out for them with grandiose expectations. Perhaps they'll summit the thing by sunset. A day later, after having walked nonstop, the mountain is still on the horizon and their expectations have mollified. They want merely to camp in its shadow.

Jessup and his father had not yet given up entirely, but the germ of surrender was beginning to incubate, at least for Jessup— he had less at stake in the endeavor and was becoming less certain that the healer's words were true.

"What if we kill him," said Jessup, "and the comet comes, and you stay the same?"

Rondell shook his head. "Let's not think like that."

Hope is a great motivator, but it's a great deceiver too. They continued on in unwarranted pursuit, aiming at any clue afforded to them, asking strangers with black eyes for information that seemed laughable.

"Redhead? Sure. There's a town of them. Three days north of here. By a lake filled with mermaids, each one with the nicest pair a titties you've ever seen."

Sad thing was, while these fibs came, Rondell listened intently as if he was audience to some kind of sermonizing.

"Hear that," he'd say to Jessup. "North. Just three days."

And Jessup would sort of lead him on.

But, his patience for all this was wearing thin.

You have to understand how rare a thing a father was. The whole world seemed to be against their existing. It was hard enough to keep your shadow on the outside: to be surrounded by prey was irrational.

Rondell was the only father Jessup or Rondell knew by name. If you met a man, clearly he'd been begotten, but the begetter was always off attending to his own affairs, often leaving behind sleepless women and hate-filled children, and Jessup was deeply indebted to his father for proving an anomaly in that regard. The man was his hero.

They lived together in a hut surrounded by vast acres of grapefruit groves that Rondell and Jessup would harvest for grapefruit moonshine. They did this not to act as suppliers for folks, but, rather, they hoarded alcohol and lived a kind of loose life deeply hid away from the world in their thorny labyrinth of grapefruit trees.

Jessup's mother had died in childbirth.

He'd never seen a picture of her, but Rondell would often describe her.

"Prettier than the stars when you're drunk."

Deep, high praise for such an alcoholic.

Some days, for no reason, Rondell would wake Jessup up and tell him, "Let's celebrate your ma today." And that meant they'd drink more than usual, and he'd sing half-remembered tunes they used to dance to, and he'd show Jessup blankets she made.

It was after one of these celebrations that Rondell passed out in the grass and the redheaded boy gobbled his shadow. Jessup caught a glimpse of the thief tarrying off after the deed was done.

He gave chase, following him down the thorny tree rows, but couldn't catch him.

When he returned to his father, Rondell sat Indian style bawling.

"I've lost your mother and now I've lost my shadow and it's not fair," he said. "It's not fair how life's treated me."

Once Jessup had shaken some of the moonshine from his brain, he took Rondell to see the healer.

Then their real journey began, but now it was beginning to seem pointless to Jessup, and Rondell sensed this, and he tried to explain:

"I got a hooker once. It's the only thing I can compare it to. It was in this botched place called Boys' Town, a bunch of stinky streets with bedroom doors that opened right onto it. Little bedrooms, they were, and whores stood in those doorways. Most of them had diseases, I guess, but I still went inside, and the room was the smell of old sex and lavender and I got lost in the bad magic of it, fell into the bed with my whore and we did a gross amount of sex. Maybe hours. But for all the thrashing and all the wanting and all desirousness that dwelled in me, I could not seem to finish. We were yanking and snatching and tugging and what have you. And the whore was laughing at me, and she called in a friend, and I thought that might help, the indecency of it all. But outside the sun rose. And at some point I just gave up. Right now is like being in that room and knowing that it won't end how I want it to."

"Can you stand?" Jessup asked.

"I can try, but I just wanna fucking sleep."

Jessup helped lift his father from the earth. Shouldering most of his weight, he led him, exhausted, across that desert.

Days went on like that.

And then the comet came.

They watched it streak the sky with sadness in their hearts. A decapitated head of magic being lobbed across the sky.

Where were they even then?

And Jessup addressed his father.

"We can't get you all the way home like this." It was the next morning and Jessup was bearing the brunt of Rondell's load. His feet worked over the grasses and brambles while his father's slogged through them.

"Leave me, I suppose. I don't want to drag you down."

Jessup couldn't catch shade: his father had barely slept. "I can't leave you, but we'll need to detour."

"Detour? Add to the journey?"

Jessup let Rondell slip from his shoulder, let him rest on the ground.

Rondell fanned himself with a hand.

"Nearby," said Jessup, "there's a town with a machine that makes shadows, kind of. I've only heard about it. They take trade, I don't know what, and we don't have much. But I think we have to try. Get you some sleep."

Rondell closed his eyes. "How far?"

"Maybe a day."

"And home? The goats?"

"Maybe three."

Rondell opened his eyes again, looked off at the clouds, smiled as much as he could. "It's worth a shot," he said.

Cellmates

For hours after Murk died, Mira and Bale stayed silent.

The only noise was their pained breathing.

"I DIDN'T WANT it like this," Mira said.

"I know."

"CAN YOU UNTIE my hands?"

"I can try."

BALE WRIGGLED ON the floor to her and she picked at the ropes.

"I can't get it."

She draped her arms over his shoulders.

She pressed her face to his face.

There were dead bodies all around them.

There was blood and the gunshot smells.

But inside that cell, their shared warmth was dazzling.

• • •

"You think we'll die in here?"

The puddle of blood around Clover discolored, the plasma separating.

"I'm not sure."

They dozed in and out. Dreamed with their eyes open. The shock of the world kept them living in fear. Kept reality blinking on and off like a strobe light—revealing brief snippets, scattering infinite shadows. Promising naught but captivity.

In Need of Sleep

Bale's eyes opened.

Had something woken him?

"Hello?" he heard the faint call. Some parch-throated holler.

"Mira," Bale said. "Wake up." He gently shimmied her shoulder with his foot.

She stirred, opened her eyes uneasily seemed confused by her surroundings until she saw Bale's face. "What?"

"Do you hear it?"

The quiet so spare it took a while to be certain.

"I don't hear anything."

They waited, their eyes out of focus, striving at something with their ears.

"Hello?" it came again—their ears like dry tongues against a form of wet in the noise of it.

"That?" said Bale.

"Maybe?" Could Mira be certain of anything sitting in that rookery of death, in that nest of lifeless bodies akimbo?

Bale got to his feet, "In here," he screamed. "Hello! In here!"

He leaned his shoulder into the bars, his scalp grazing the cold of one.

Two men showed at the door. One with a face that Bale knew.

"You," Bale said. "I know you." He strained toward him, all of his strength behind the gesture.

The recognized man shook his head. "I don't think so." He made some sound that wasn't language with his throat, "I don't know prisoners."

"Jessup," said Bale. "From the train, you shadow thiever."

Jessup went gentle in his eyes. "Oh yeah," he said. "That's right."

"Let us out of here," Bale said.

Jessup touched his forehead, rubbed a bit where Bale's barrel had been. "I don't know, son. Think if you were in my position." He scrutinized the distance, the way a preacher might when saying something hard to the congregation. "I just come to a town of death, and you think I should let its only prisoners free?" His eyes back on Bale.

"Look," said Bale, "I coulda blasted you to death and didn't."

Jessup and Rondell conversed in whispers. "Sorry, son," Jessup said. The plaintive silence of an implied go fuck yourself. "It just don't seem right." And they made to leave.

"But you *owe* me," said Bale, his voice cracking against the word *owe* so it sounded the way an animal might chirp it.

Jessup and Rondell didn't answer. Only disappeared from the doorway. The thing just a rectangle of pitiful light.

Wildly, Bale's mind spun to produce some sort of incentive. "The machine," he hollered. "I bet you're looking for it." Bale spoke to Mira, "You know where it is, right?"

"Right outside," Mira said.

In an inside-only voice, "See how it worked?"

"Kind of."

Bale yelled as loud as he could. "We can get your dad fixed up on the machine," he said. "He can use it for sleeping."

A few moments passed. Long shapeless ones. The light in the doorway. A sort of signal of the end.

Bale hung his head, all his energy dripping invisibly from his disheveled Mohawk, draining out like woe.

But then, miraculously, Jessup returned.

Cut the Ropes

Mira hugged Jessup and Rondell when they unlocked the cell door, the stink of this embrace impossible to convey with words, but you could almost hold the way it smelled, all that traveling and discomfort. Could regard it like coinage.

"You can show us the machine?" Jessup said.

"Yeah," said Mira. "Just hang on." She crossed the room, reached out and pulled the machete free from Doc's face and held it—old blood dried against it like wax, Doc's eyes open, staring at some point beyond any true place.

"Now hold the fuck on," said Jessup. "We did y'all a solid," he said. So much fear in his voice Mira could've sharpened the machete against it. "We've saved you from in that cell." Dead Clover lay bled out there, his nudity going bloat.

Mira was confused until she realized the weapon she held. "No," she said. She rolled her eyes. "Bale, turn around."

Bale did, eyeing Jessup as he turned. "Fucking pussy," Bale said to Jessup, and Mira cut the rope from his wrists and Bale shook his hands and stretched and thought about taking fists to Jessup's ribs.

But Mira grabbed Jessup by a hand, led him and his father outside into the day's harsh sun. The machine was covered by its tarp. She untied a cord at the base of it and pulled the thing free. The legs and arms dangled from their hooks, rocking gently with the inertia of their reveal. "Have at it," she said, and Jessup helped his father to the shade on the sand, and he slurped up a bit of it and rolled off into a deep slumber and Jessup smiled goofily down at him, pawed his silver wisps of hair.

Mira and Bale went back inside the jail. Murk's blood had gone back to red. He slumped on the ground in the mess of it.

"We should bury him," Bale said. "I think that was the word."

"No," said Mira.

"It was something like that," Bale said. "Digging holes for the dead. Covering 'em with dirt."

"That's the right word. I'm just not burying him." She touched Murk's butchered up hair. "Some other time, maybe. But right now, he can stay this way." Mira leaned down and claimed her Dutch oven. "A world with two suns," she said to Murk. She frowned up at Bale. "It's time to go home."

Home

"That was Jessup?" Mira said.

"Yes."

"And that was Jessup's dad?"

"It was."

"And the redhead is dead."

"And the comet came and went."

They moved across the same terrain that they'd traversed to get to the Town of Lost Souls, but they stayed silent for the most part, passing the landscape with contemplative eyes.

Mira carried her Dutch oven in front of her like some wounded thing, and the lid rattled metallically.

THEY CAME TO Mira's home the next morning, and it looked the same as it always did—a shaggy thing hunkered back in the camouflage of ancient tree limbs—but there were a few additions. A lifeless chicken rested in the yard, its feathers yellowed out with death, kicked free by whatever, the wings sprawled in skeletal fashion, plumules drifting in the morning light, clung up on grass blades like frosting. Beside that bird, a young nanny goat with no shadow wandered bleating odd noises, stepping spasmodically, kicking chicken feathers.

As they approached, they saw Mira's mother in her chair, her feet propped on the ancient TV, deeply asleep, drool dangling from her bottom lip, shiny like candy.

Mira chucked her pot, and it banged on the lawn, and her mother slept through it, so Mira walked to her. "Wake up," Mira said. She shifted her weight. "Wake up!" But still her mother slept.

Mira shook her. Grabbed her by her shoulders and rocked her hard back and forth until her mother's eyes opened, shocked and red. "Mira," she said. "You're home."

"How'd you get by, Mom? How'd you sleep?"

"What?"

"Without me here to hunt you shadows?"

"I don't . . ."

Mira lifted her mother and dragged her toward the goat pen, her mother's feet kicking dirt as she dragged her, and Mira called to Bale. "Get me a goat." The world sped up.

"What?" Bale said.

"Get me a *fucking* goat, Bale. From the pen. If you want to live here you have to help me. So get me a fucking goat." Mira's voice full the way oceans are full.

Bale ran off to the goat pen and struggled back a goat that brayed and fought him.

Mira looked down at her mother, at her chalky face and victim-thick eyes. "You're gonna suck this goat shadow off the ground and I'm gonna watch you suck it and that's the way it's gonna be from now on and it's gonna be fair and I won't hear you say otherwise."

Her mother's mouth dropped into some peculiar configuration and her eyes seemed spat into. "What I ever do to you?"

"Nothing, Mom. You didn't do shit. And Joe Clover didn't either. And Murk didn't get shot. And Bale's brother's not dead. Because everything's fair. So tell yourself whatever you need to hear, but make it fair just like everything else. Make up some story or some God to help you understand it, and believe it, because once you're done making it fair, I'm gonna watch you suck that goat shadow and then we're never going to talk about it again. It'll just be a thing you do. Every day before sunset. We'll get you a bed out by the pen, and that's where you'll sleep, or we'll figure out some better way, but I'm not hunting shadow for you ever again."

Mira's mother was almost offended by the goat Bale restrained and she made to cough up her mantra, "It's not . . ."

But Mira just screamed, "Make it fair!" And she lowered her face so close to her mother's it seemed she might bite her eyes. "Is it fair?" Mira asked, and the few inches between them seemed to fill with imaginary sparks of Mira's hatred.

Sometimes the space between two things can only be measured with emotions.

A language was invented then.

In Mira's eyes.

It lived just long enough to convey one message then disappeared from all creation.

"Is it *fair*?" Mira asked again, her eyes now calmed.

Her mother hesitated, but lowered her face. Toward the

shadow. And started sucking it up. Swallowed so much the goat panicked, snorted shrill, but just before the whole shadow was gone, Mira pulled her mother away, let her lay back and fall asleep in the grass, and Bale let the goat free and it stumbled around confused.

Bale rubbed his forearms where the cuffs of his shirtsleeves reached and started to laugh.

"What's funny?" said Mira.

"Jessup," Bale said. "We didn't tell him the redhead was dead."

Mira walked to Bale and they stood and were quiet and Bale put his arm around her.

There was a sleep-deprived goat, bleating, stumbling queerly. There was a worn-out woman passed out in the morning grass. There was a boy holding a girl, and the girl didn't cast shadow. But other than that, everything seemed just fine.

Acknowledgments

Sip wouldn't be possible without the work of Roy Sorensen. My dear friend Cameron Pierce. My amazing agent, Bill Clegg. And my phenomenal family. Also my editor, Mark Doten—who is a godsend and a genius—and everyone else at SOHO. Especially Kevin "Bird Shirt" Murphy (who I've never met but known forever), Rachel Kowal, Abby Koski, and Bronwen Hruska.